THE BUS

THE BUS

Adam Pottle

QUATTRO BOOKS

The publication of *The Bus* has been generously supported by the Canada Council for the Arts and the Ontario Arts Council.

 Canada Council   Conseil des arts
for the Arts   du Canada

 ONTARIO ARTS COUNCIL
CONSEIL DES ARTS DE L'ONTARIO
an Ontario government agency
un organisme du gouvernement de l'Ontario

Author's photograph: Kristen Hergott
Cover Painting: Robin Adair
Cover design: Natasha Shaikh
Typography: Zile Liepins
Editor: Luciano Iacobelli

Library and Archives Canada Cataloguing in Publication

Pottle, Adam, author
        The Bus / Adam Pottle.

ISBN 978-1-988254-28-9 (paperback)

        I. Title.

PS8631.O7746B87 2016   C813'.6   C2016-906370-4

Published by Quattro Books Inc.
Toronto
quattrobooks.ca

Printed in Canada

For those deemed unworthy of life:

275,000, and those before and since.

Reich Leader Bouhler and Dr. Brandt are charged with the responsibility of expanding the authority of physicians, to be designated by name, to the end that patients considered incurable according to the best available human judgment of their state of health, can be granted a mercy death.

-Adolf Hitler, October 1939 (backdated to September first)

NADJA

I roll my head to one side and peer across the ward. The sun's beginning to rise: I can see the outlines of the curtains. In the daytime they're stiff and white, like used tissues. But right now they're soft, the incoming light softly framing them. It's almost time to get up.

I hold my hand up to my face. The bandage has loosened. The blood's dried to a crust. I tap it with my finger: a few tings of pain, like my hand is a bell. The nurses still haven't given me a shot.

I balance myself on my elbows and look around. Some of the others shift beneath their sheets. Silke and Judith and Anna all shift, as though some imp or golem has slid along the floor and knocked the bottoms of their beds. It's easy to imagine their dreams being the same. I imagine their dreams are pantomimes of their intellects, full of goopy gulping noises and vehement gibberish and people getting stuck and hitting themselves in the head, a poorly written Chaplin film.

Silke grunts and jerks her sheet around her. Even during sleep time, every minute on this ward is loaded with bitching and comedy. At any given moment, anyone, due to a perceived change in the ward's temperature, or a stray hair landing on a pillow, or an imagined grimace from the girl across the aisle, may swing her fists, or cower and tuck herself under her sheets, or take you by the shoulders and, in a meandering, nonsensical monologue, explain why the *Schweinstaffel* took her away and put her here, her words a delirious mixture of Goethe and Walter Mehring.

I hum "Bake, Bake a Cake." Silke's mouth is open. I can see her small teeth. I'm surprised there's no meat on them. I lie back down. As I settle my head on my pillow, Judith gets up and walks to the bathroom. At least twice a night, she gets up and washes her hands and face. The poor girl, with her bottom-heavy body and slanted eyes. She talks to her mother in there too. She's become embarrassed to do so in front of everyone. It's amusing that an idiot possesses some sense of dignity.

LEOPOLD

Aunt Minna stands above me, clutching my head like a crystal ball. I'm sitting in the middle of a small room. It feels underground – the ceiling bears down on me. We could be in her basement, though I don't remember this room. A yellow light hangs from the ceiling. It sways from side to side, dragging its light into and out of the dark corners of the room.

Aunt Minna's mouth is tight. Her eyes have lost their colour. Her pupils have dilated all the way out.

"Stay still," she says.

Her words emerge from one corner of her mouth. Her fingernails slide across my scalp. My head feels light, as though her nail has unzipped my head, letting out all the tension. She taps my temple with a long fingernail.

"It might burst," she says. "Don't get any on me."

I hear a loud scratch, a groan. I grunt and open my eyes and see the high, grey ceiling of the ward. The yellow light dissolves, and the edges of my vision tremble and settle. I roll sideways and remove the wadded sheet from my mouth and lift it close to my face. No blood. I wasn't asleep long. I look around the room. A short time ago, the boy was wailing. He's quiet now.

The dream rocks and sloshes in my head like wine in a jug. I shut my eyes and try to keep it still. Aunt Minna's hands were cold. Her voice was even deeper than usual. I wonder if, like my seizures, her deafness has worsened, and if it's thickened her unusual accent. If it has, the *Schutzstaffel* might've picked her up by now.

I push my tongue between my teeth and feel the rough, meaty latticework of scar tissue. Everything's magnified in the mouth – the chewed, uneven tip. My tongue feels forked.

I carefully turn my head. The others pretend to be asleep. A few of them huddle into themselves. Many of them shiver and shift – the hospital's blankets are much too thin. There are several windows in the ward. Dusky light teeters at the edges of the curtains.

A few beds down from me, the boy, Thomas, starts to wail again. The sedative's worn off. He shrieks for a moment and starts to buck up off the bed and swing his arms. Like a swarm of flies hovers above him. Several men groan. I hunch over and cover my ears. It's not enough.

A man I don't know says, "Someone please shut him up."

At the end of the room, Sebastian, the librarian, turns onto his side and pushes the blanket off himself.

"No!"

At the other end, Frederick jerks up from his bed. His voice rasps against the walls of my skull. Even in the dark, I can see his coarse face.

"You stay where you are," he says to Sebastian.

"The boy needs help. He trusts me."

"Just go already," someone says. "Whoever, anyone. He's keeping us up."

"No," Frederick says. "Don't move."

Frederick's mouth makes grey movements in the dark. He points his finger and jabs it in Sebastian's direction. His finger leaves grey streaks on the air. Thomas has propped himself on his knees and is now beating the metal rails of his bed. His arms whip down and jar against the white rails. His voice floods my ears and spikes through my head. In the bed next to mine, Peter ducks under his pillow. The other men in the room face away from Thomas. Their thin blankets flap.

"Goddamn it." Frederick throws off his blanket.

Sebastian stands. "He hates you," he says. "You don't know what to do with him."

"You get the hell away from him."

The ward's door opens, and two male nurses enter. "Stay there," they say to Frederick. They run over to Thomas. One of them seizes Thomas by the shoulders and forces him still. He says, "Should we inject him now or later?"

Thomas' voice swings into a register I thought only babies could reach. I bite my lip and groan and squeeze my ears. The second nurse injects him in the leg. His limbs stop shaking. His voice shrinks into gentle sobs. One of the nurses looks at me and blinks.

"Should we just get them up now?" he says.

"Let's wait a little longer."

They watch Thomas for a moment. When he stops making noises, they leave. Frederick nods at them. He glances at Sebastian, who's sat back down on his bed.

"You stay away from him. No more groping him."

Frederick makes a face like he's biting down on grit. Sebastian sighs and turns onto his other side. I lie back down. The thin light from the windows has begun to stretch across the ceiling.

EMMERICH

I never meant to, not to Papa, we were playing, I know I'm too big I shouldn't have jumped on him but he was laughing and pushing me, Klaus had gone to town for the day he couldn't say anything couldn't stop me, so when we'd put the horses back in the stable their tails like a woman's hair swinging Papa splashed me with water and roughed my hair laughing he turned and I laughing saw his back his back looked exactly the same way as when I was six when I jumped on and held his neck he ran around carrying me said we're a couple of cowboys or maybe he said knights, his back was so big and open I jumped on again, his legs went hard he went stiff under me he shouted something popped in his back and he fell, god he said my back my fucking back, swatting me away from him I bent down crying his eyes heaving like Old Lizard's dark eyes when he broke his leg or was it Gibraltar's eyes when she got caught in the wire, I went to pick him up no Emmerich get away get your mother, Papa, for Christ's sake get your mother I ran back to the house feeling wind under my arms, my shoes felt loose I fixed my feet down steadying jumping over the woodpile, Old Lizard had to go when he broke his leg that means Papa had to shoot him took him where I couldn't see but I could still hear and I cried thinking about the shot going into Old Lizard's head, I shouted Mama Mama almost ran her over when she came to the door, Emmerich, I cried hard, what is it where's your father had to finish crying before I could tell, because of Old Lizard because of Gibraltar who wasn't shot but ran away after she came unstuck, Mama called Doctor Waller and he came to where Papa lay by the stable, I kept the insects away, Doctor Waller needed my help getting Papa home, I need you to pick him up Emmerich Doctor Waller said I tucked my hands underneath Papa made my hands flat on his chest and legs, I lifted him feeling that he didn't want me to lift him so I didn't say anything and I put him on the old wagon, Mama watched the back wheel that was your grandfather's wagon she said if it falls off you might have to carry him Emmerich, I walked beside Papa saying to Doctor Waller I didn't mean to yes okay Emmerich, Papa's face red from lying in the sun, grass and dirt caught in his hair, he nodded to me yes don't touch me Emmerich don't touch me it was an accident yes don't touch me

nobody here asks me, they're scared of me, I don't like that they're scared of me, I sit at the window and watch the hill behind the hospital, sometimes a dog or a boy runs past sometimes a group of boys walks past and looks up at me, they smile but they don't get too close to the building, when I move they run away, I get dust on my feet, the chairs are too small my knees bend and my feet flop off the end of the bed, I asked for another blanket to put over my feet but everybody gets one, the nurses are smaller than me, Frederick comes too close to me and puts his hand on my shoulder, Emmerich he says I hate his voice look how big you are why don't you just take something break a window and leave why don't you just strangle them look at your hands, I don't say anything, he walks away, idiot he says with that much size you know what I could do, Frederick doesn't care he takes blankets from other men and spits on the floor, he yells at the boy when he has fits I don't say anything

when Klaus came back from town he woke me up in the middle of the night took me outside behind the stable his nails skidding pinching my neck, my toes scruffy with dust, wearing only my shirt and drawers, I wanted to say something but I didn't I said his name, he put me on my knees the night tasted like iron, why he said why don't they get it, you nearly break Papa's back how can they still put up with you, a knife made a blue flash in the moonlight had a thick runnel, he held out my arm stay still he said and made three long cuts, I tried to pull away, even though I'm taller than Klaus by five inches he's bigger than me, he shook my arm, this is for what you did to Papa, I cried out, Emmerich be quiet, he spat on my arm pressed the knife against my cheek jerked it back opened the skin beneath my eye, what is it about you he said what do I have to do, I touch the open skin fold it back like paper, I think he was about to cry I'd never seen him cry before, he cut me again on the arm the knife flashed again, what do I have to do flashcutflash flashcutflash do you realize Emmerich do you realize flashcutflash flashcutflash

the boy flattens beneath his blanket, I don't like that they inject him when he's screaming the room seems smaller when he screams

JUDITH

I cradle the soap in my hands. The water's not hot enough. The sink is too old. Full of rust and scratches. I try to scrape it away. It gathers under my thumbnail. I dry my hands on my skirt. Everyone else has used the towel.

They still haven't replaced the mirror. I stoop to see myself in the cracked bits sticking out the bottom. My eyes move in different directions. My nose is flat. "Everyone wants a nose like yours," Mama said. "It's the ones with the big noses that get in trouble." I stand up straight. The mirror's wooden back is broken and splintered.

Several feet above the toilet is a vent opening onto the outside world. Wire has been nailed across it. The sunlight feels cold. I cradle the soap. The nurses will wake everyone up soon, and today's shower day. I don't want to share the soap again. I fold it into my skirt.

"Judith."

"Nothing, Mama."

"What are you doing? Judith."

"No."

"You know it's not right to steal. You need to put that back."

I hold the soap to my nose and breathe. I see fresh green.

"The voice of the Lord is upon the waters, Mama."

"Oh Judith."

"You said I should keep myself clean. The voice of the Lord is upon many waters. That's how people will take me seriously." I smell the soap again. I hug it to my chest and shut my eyes. "What do I do?"

"Don't whine, Judith. Nobody likes whiners, whether they're afflicted or not."

"But what do I do?"

"Shush. You must ask for forgiveness."

"I can keep this?"

"You must pray."

"Right now?"

"Right now."

I lower my head. My hair slips down. It needs to be cut.

"People say He won't hear me."

"He'll hear you."

"They're smarter than me. Nadja doesn't pray."

"They're ignorant. Go on, Judith."

"He'll hear me? Even me?"

"Yes."

I bow my head. "Dear Lord, I am sorry for having offended thee. I humbly beg your forgiveness for taking the soap."

"Amen."

"Amen. Is that okay?"

"That'll do."

"I can keep this, then?"

"Don't tell anyone."

I roll the soap into my skirt. Someone comes into the washroom. I pull the soap up into both hands. One of the nurses looks at me.

"Judith, what are you doing out of bed?"

"I had to wash my hands."

The nurse shakes her head. She says a few things about my hands being clean and tells me to come out. She holds the door open for me. Everyone is awake and talking. Nadja sits at the end of her bed. She's smiling at me. She holds her bloody hand and sings a song I don't know. I like her singing. I look at Silke, who doesn't look angry.

A nurse tells us to form a line. I look at the nurse beside me. "Today's shower day, right?"

"Yes, but you won't be showering here. You and the others are leaving."

"We're what?"

"You're being transferred to another hospital."

"We're leaving?"

I look at Nadja. She's looking at the nurses.

"Come on, Judith," a nurse says. "Get in line."

The nurse puts her hand on my shoulder and walks with me. She puts me between two women whose names I don't know. One of them stares at the floor. The other glances around and claps her hands together.

The small, fat nurse stands at the front of the room. "Everyone, pay attention," she says. "You and some of the men in the other ward are being transferred to another clinic. The nursing staff will escort you down to the bus. They'll record your name before you get on."

"Another clinic? Where?" Anna says.

"It's in Hadamar."

"We'll be riding with the men?"

"Please leave your belongings here. There's no room on the bus. We'll send them to you later on."

"Why do we have to leave?" one of the women says.

"To make room for others."

The small nurse opens the door, and everyone walks out. I look back at the other nurse. Tears slip from my eyes.

"We haven't even showered," I say.

"It'll be fine, Judith," says the other nurse. "You can shower when you get to Hadamar."

I cry. I stop walking. The women behind me push me forward. I step out of the line. The small, fat nurse approaches me and points.

"What do you have in your hands?"

She reaches for the soap. I turn away. She grabs me by the shoulder. I skip away and fall onto one of the beds and curl up tight. Two or three nurses fight to sit me up. I cry and ask Mama to come back. I know she doesn't like it when I cry, but I can't help it.

SEBASTIAN

One of the nurses carries Thomas out of the ward. The boy's soft, bed-ruffled head and skinny legs flop over his arms. The rest of us are told to walk in line. Frederick obeys, of course. Stands at the head of the line and shouts orders to the rest of us. As though obedience demonstrates sanity.

As we begin to leave the ward, Leopold accidentally bumps into Martin. Martin hollers at him for walking too close and makes a fist and clubs him on the head. Leopold cries out and cringes and claps both hands over his head. The poor man. He's said that any little strike hurts and echoes for eternity. Frederick tells Martin to shut up and nods to the nurses to continue.

I'm last in line. The others trudge ahead of me. A few of them are still drugged; they pull their feet along the floor, their shoes scraping and squeaking. When I come to the door, I say to the nurse, "Will they have books at this new clinic?" He makes a face like the question is ludicrous.

We walk to the end of the building's east wing and, in two parallel single files, go down the stairs. Our footsteps clatter on the concrete, and as we descend, the stairwell fills with what sounds like acrid splashing noises. In the lobby at the bottom, we find several women. Many of them turn away when they see us. Some of the men, including Frederick, start toward them; the nurses shove them back. "Get on the other side of the room and stay there," they say. "I just want to talk," says one of the men. A nurse says, "Stay there or we'll beat the shit out of you."

We huddle against the wall on the right. There are small windows in the clinic's entrance, over which cage wire has been fastened. Beyond them I see nothing.

One of the nurses says, "When the bus arrives, the women will go on first, then the men. You will be watched closely. If any of you try to run away, we will beat you. Do you understand?" Frederick nods and glances back at the rest of us. His eyes are like discarded tires. I watch Thomas sedated in the nurse's arms. His little pink tongue rests on his lip.

MICHAEL

I have one more bite and push away my plate. Yellowness spreads from the perforated yolks and shores up against the bread. The edges of the perforations assume a skin-like translucence, like blisters. I wash out my mouth with coffee. I'm alone in the cafeteria. I hold my coffee between both hands. Outside the smoke has assumed its familiar perch in the sky: a black arch hovering above Hadamar. Ewald is downstairs, preparing the ovens. From the second floor, I feel their heat.

"Good morning, Doctor Würfel."

Isabella sits across from me. She spreads honey on a piece of bread. I nod at her.

"Congratulations," she says. "Usually I'm the first one up. Everyone here seems to love their sleep. But you beat me here this morning."

She tears her bread in half.

"I take pride in being the first one up," she says. "It gives me a feeling of preparedness for whatever the day brings. It seems especially helpful when you work with unpredictable people." She takes a bite and swallows it immediately. "You look pale," she says.

"I didn't sleep well."

"You were thinking about the shower room? Today's your day, isn't it?"

I nod.

"And you're nervous."

"I haven't run patient intake on my own yet, much less the shower room."

"You've done intakes before."

"Not on this scale."

"How many patients today?"

"At least forty."

"You know how to operate the shower room, don't you?"

"Of course I do. It's just the act itself."

"Yes." Isabella eats the other half of her bread. "Ewald drinks each evening," she says.

"Mm."

"I don't know if his is the more difficult job. You'll be fine. Doctor Berner wouldn't have asked you to do it if he thought you couldn't handle it."

I sip my coffee, which is getting cold. The smoke has begun to widen and spread across the sky.

"How long have you been a nurse?" I say.

"About eight years."

"So since the *Führer's* been in power. Have you been in Hadamar the whole time?"

"No. I worked in Munich before, and then when the Party began its new program, they transferred me here."

"And what's been your experience in that time?"

"How do you mean?"

"With the sterilizations, the busses, the shower rooms. What do you think of it all?"

Isabella drinks her juice. "I don't think about it," she says. "It's a job. It needs to be done."

"But you've convinced yourself of that. How?"

"The usual reasons."

"Usual reasons."

"Are you having difficulty convincing yourself, Doctor?"

"No. It's just a bit of anxiety about having to perform."

"You won't be alone. We'll all be there to help you."

"I know. I'm grateful for that."

Isabella rises from the table and gets another piece of bread; she spreads honey on it and begins eating.

"You don't look like you're thirty," she says.

"I'm thirty-one."

"You don't look it. Seems that's more common. People looking younger."

"Hm. A product of *rassenhygiene*?"

Isabella chuckles and glances out the window.

"It doesn't feel like April, does it?" she says.

"Snow's almost gone."

"It's grey but hot. It's disorienting."

"Be nice to go outside soon."

"Yes, it can be stifling in here."

"I might go later today. Afterwards."

NADJA

We all hear the bus swing into the yard. Everyone perks up their heads like a roused audience. The nurses open the door, and we all go out, hanging our tired heads. The air rises around us. I gather it in my hands and squeeze it and wiggle my fingers: cool relief on my bandaged hand. A nurse says, "Is that it? Just the one today?" Another says, "We'll have to stuff them in."

We're led single file up to the bus. The men stay behind, watching. They probably haven't seen a woman for days – they look at us like famished sailors at a feast. One of them tries to touch Anna. A nurse beats the man away, and Anna huddles up with Kristina, whose condition I don't know. Our feet stir the dirt. I kick some up and inhale it and hold it at the back of my throat. I finger my bandaged hand, the dark crust of blood.

The bus is long and painted the colour of mushrooms, and except for the front window, all the other windows are similarly painted. I haven't been on a bus before. The painted windows conceal who's inside. It feels like a theatrical set piece.

Judith won't stop crying. She hides her face in her skirt. Some of the others tell her to shut up. I put my hand on her shoulder and help her forward. A male nurse stands at the door, holding a clipboard.

"Your names?"

"I'm Eva, and she's Maria."

He reads the list. "Eva? Maria what?"

"Schwartz."

Judith looks at me. I cock my eyebrows.

"I don't see Maria Schwartz here. What's your last name, Eva?"

"Schömmelmeyer. I guess we're not supposed to be here, then. Should we go back inside?"

"I don't see you on the list."

"Must be a mistake. We'll just go back in then."

"No, you don't!"

The fat troll waddles up. Her white armpits are soaked. Her breathing sounds like a dog having a nightmare.

"Damn you, Nadja."

She gives the man our names. Her face is cobbled. A single hair curls out of her chin. I want to pull it and straighten it with pomade.

"You'll miss me?" I say.

"Like hell."

"Come on. I broke the tension. You smiled."

She squints and glares. Her compressed face makes me think of squeezing a sandwich together.

"All you did was cause trouble. Look at your hand."

"Piss off. She was having a fit. She ran up and bit me. It wasn't my fault."

"You deserved it either way. Get on the bus."

"My hand's been bothering me. Will I get a tetanus shot when I get there? Maybe a rabies shot too?"

"Go!"

"Jesus. So you'll just let my hand fall off?"

She tilts her head.

"Goddamn fatty," I say. "Why am I here, anyway? There's nothing wrong with me. When will I be released?"

She pushes us both inside the bus. Judith trips on the steps. I help her up. She bawls and grips her elbow.

"Get up," I say. "Come on, you're okay." I lead her forward. "That was a great fall. I bet Mr. Chaplin would be proud."

The driver doesn't look at us. A curtain separates him from the seats in the back. We move through the curtain and sit down. The bus is dim and moist. The seats smell like mildew. Judith tries to look out the painted windows. She drops her forehead against the glass and slaps the back of the seat in front of us. The nurse at the door tells her to be quiet. She makes a noise like a jammed engine. I pat her leg. "Sorry, Judith," I say. "I tried."

The others come onto the bus. One of the nurses rolls the curtain back; I study the clinic through the front window. It seems small from the outside. I'm surprised there are so many windows. Some of the men kick dirt at each other. I touch my aching hand. I think it's about eight o'clock in the morning.

LEOPOLD

The front of the bus looks like the snout of a starved shepherd. The women file onto the bus. Their sweat smells different than our sweat. I watch their feet. Behind them I see trees. I didn't notice them when I first arrived here. The light and the air and the dirt and the noise are extravagant. I cough and shut my eyes and keep my distance from Martin. Everyone's voices burrow into my ears. I hum and try to match their pitch, try to overcome it, like when Aunt Minna was baking and she dropped the old heavy pan onto the table and it didn't bother her at all, and I heard her from my little room in the basement and even down there the noise was too much, and she knew it, so I had to hum.

One of the men says, "I'm not getting on there."

"Yes, you are."

"Schuster will find me."

"No one's going to find you, *Herr* Holtz. Look, all the windows are painted. Nobody will see you."

Holtz sobs. I think he bumps against me. I open my eyes.

"I couldn't get the money," he says. "I've been in here the whole time. My family doesn't have it, and I'm the only one who can work."

A nurse waves to him and leads him by the shoulder.

Holtz says, "My father once filled a wheelbarrow full of money and took it out to the back and burned it. I admired him when he did that. Thousands and thousands of *Reich* marks. I felt rich."

"Come on. All of you."

One of the nurses grips my arm. His thumb skids up my elbow. The women are all on the bus. Frederick leads the men. His short hair is rough like a horsehair brush. A short ways ahead of me, Holtz steps out of the line. A nurse grabs him. He twists away from the nurse and tries to run. Another nurse seizes Holtz from behind, tying up his arms. Holtz shouts and kicks. The first nurse shoves his legs aside and punches him in the stomach. I close my eyes. The blows continue. Holtz shouts. Everyone else quiets down. The light on my eyelids is smudged and angry. Martin's punch still rattles in my head. I concentrate on keeping the light still.

Someone leads me forward. "There's four steps," he says. "Lift your leg. Take the steps." I step up. I slip past a curtain. The bus bristles around me. I sit down. I haven't walked deep into the bus. I open my eyes and see the window, painted a stifling, dusty colour. Across the aisle from me, Holtz slumps in his seat and wipes his bloody nose. I close my eyes. Everyone's voices clatter.

SEBASTIAN

I stand in the aisle, the curtain at my back. Before me, awash in a swampy light, sits a breathtaking panorama of human folly. A festering Brueghel portrait, the sum of humanity's burdens and fears, as determined by the *Reich*. And I must sit among them.

"Move."

A nurse points up the aisle. Another one stands behind him, glaring.

"I think all the seats are taken."

"Now."

"Look. The seats are full."

Having been aggravated by Holtz, they want no more nonsense. They push me forward; I stumble up and find Martin occupying a seat by himself. I hesitate. One of the nurses lunges at me. I sit down. Martin grunts and whips his hand into my face.

"Jesus, Martin."

"Away."

His knuckles clack across my temple. His long fingernails click against my forehead.

"For God's sake. There's nowhere else to sit."

He whines and slides onto his back and kicks me in the ribs. I lurch back into the aisle. The nurses stare at me. I move toward the back of the bus. All the seats are crowded with two or three people except Thomas'; he sits by himself. Before I can get close, Frederick sticks his leg out; I step over it. He pushes me.

I sit down beside Thomas. He lies loosely on the seat. His eyes are glassy. I take his shoulders and set him upright.

"Hey!" Frederick stands and looks at the nurses and points at me. "He can't sit there. You know he'll fondle that boy."

"I'm not hurting anything," I say. "He's all by himself. There's no room anywhere else."

"Go to the back," a nurse says. "That boy needs to sit alone."

"Why? He's sedated."

"Because you'll rub your hands all over him," Frederick says.

"Shut up, Frederick. Look, he'll fall off the seat. There's nothing keeping him here."

"Go to the back," the nurse says.

"Go to the back, you sick bastard."

"Come on. This is ridiculous. There's no room."

The nurse stands and walks toward me.

"For God's sake."

I get up and walk to the back of the bus. Emmerich sits alone.

He fills almost the entire seat by himself. In the seat across from him, a woman and a man sit. The man looks up at me and extends his arm possessively over the woman.

"Can you move a little?" I say to Emmerich.

He looks at me and then slides a few inches closer to the window.

"Thank you."

He nods. "I've never been on a bus," he says. "I wasn't when they brought me here. That's weird, isn't it? Leaving differently?"

The driver pulls the curtain across the front of the bus and closes the door. Four male nurses stand at the front. One of them steps forward and says, "Everyone, quiet down. Quiet, be quiet. Stay where you are. As you've been told, your time at Scheuern has ended. You're now being transferred to Hadamar. Please remain seated while we're driving. Don't make too much noise. When we arrive, you'll get new clothes and a hot shower." The nurse sits down. The driver pushes the bus into gear, and the bus rolls over the bumpy lot.

Emmerich leans close. "Hadamar. Where's Hadamar?"

"Northeast. About two and a half hours away."

Emmerich makes a face. "I live an hour from here."

He tries to look out the window. He ducks his head, trying to find a gap or a hole in the paint.

"That's outside the circle," he says.

"What circle?"

"Two and a half hours. An hour and a half past. I mean, the circle."

"The radius?"

"If it's the same direction." Emmerich glances around and bites his lip. "I don't know if my family knows. That I'm leaving."

"I'm sure the institution will notify them."

"Send a letter."

"Yes."

"What about your family?"

"I don't have any family."

"Not your mother?"

I shake my head.

Emmerich hums for a moment. "I came here two days after my mother's birthday."

"I see."

"She cried." He studies me. "We haven't really talked," he says.

"To your mother?"

"No, you and me."

"Well, there are lots of people here. Some of them don't like to talk."

"I like to talk. Sometimes." He scratches his leg. "How old are you?"

"Forty-two."

"I'm almost nineteen."

"Happy early birthday."

"In three days. What's the date today?"

"April twenty-first."

"Four days. The twenty-fifth." Emmerich nods. "Why are you here?"

"Who knows? Various reasons. According to the *Reich*."

Emmerich grunts. His green eyes narrow.

"You seem smart. You tell all those stories."

"They're children's stories. Everyone knows them."

"I like how you tell them. I like your voice."

"Thank you."

Three seats in front of us, Thomas' soft head shudders with the bus' rhythms. For a second, his hair lifts and settles, like it's sighing. Like Martin, he sits by himself, the nurses having told everyone to stay away. I cup my hands together. Emmerich starts fingering a tear in the seat. Everyone seems to drift in the swampy light.

FREDERICK

Peter slumps in his seat. His hands and arms bounce and tilt with the bus. His hands roll open like he's begging. His fingers curled and still. Useless coward. Tried to avoid the war. The emptiness plain for everyone to see. His nails and his beard and his stretching belly and his eyes like mark coins. Useless. He deserves everything he gets. Beside me two little men. Their nails as long as witches'. I hold my fist above them. They hug each other like queers. I say "You be quiet. And don't move." Sebastian sits in the back talking to the idiot. Their faces the colour of gangrene. The boy sits three rows up from him. His eyes clunk around. Seeing nothing. Sebastian kept telling everyone. His nose sliding toward me saying "Frederick's a helpless liar. It's not his fault. It's his condition. And his temper too. He can't help it." But I choose. I saw him in the washroom with Thomas. The boy's pants down. Sebastian's arm jiggling. His breath chugging chugging chugging. His fingers wrapped around the little pink prick. Stealing the boy's pleasure for himself. The boy's jaw slack. I grabbed Sebastian. He yelled. I pulled him away from the boy. "Fucking pervert." I punched him. Two orderlies came in and separated us. I said "He was violating that boy." Sebastian held up a towel and said "I was helping him clean up. Look at his pants." The boy had pissed himself. He was crying. The orderlies shook their heads. Looked at me like I was the liar. I said "Goddamn it. Goddamn you Sebastian." The boy whimpered and shuffled his feet. Sebastian walked toward him. I said "Get away from him." He said "What? Are you going to clean him up?" "Son of a bitch." I went for him. The orderly stepped in front of me and pushed me back. I tried to reach over his shoulder. Grabbed Sebastian's shirt. Sebastian tried to push my hand away. He said "Stop it will you?" The boy started wailing. The orderly told me to back off or I'd be sedated again. I said "You know he's a pervert. It says in his file doesn't it? Just let me castrate him and that'll be it." Sebastian made a face. He said "Go to hell you vicious little hobgoblin. The way you talk maybe you were touched when you were younger." A red whirring noise. "Fuck you!" Both orderlies shoved me back. The boy started smacking himself. Sebastian got to his knees and held the boy's arms. The orderlies told me to leave the bathroom. I said "Goddamn it don't leave him alone. Don't you know what he's doing to that kid? Don't you care? He's the sick one goddamn it."

JUDITH

I look into Nadja's fresh eyes and say, "They took my soap."

"Shush," she says. She puts her hands on my shoulders in the right way. Nadja's an actor. She knows how to move. She told me she took lessons in movement.

"They took my soap. And look: now my skirt is dirty."

My hands flit. They say we'll shower when we arrive, but we should've before we left. The bus is hot and filthy. People's hands and elbows butt in. Nadja is my shield, but she's too thin. I can't get used to this. I was used to my bed and my sheets and the washroom and Nadja. This is too much.

"I don't like these men," I say. "They're all dirty."

"Many men are dirty, Judith."

"There's too much noise. They don't listen."

I always listen. Many people think I don't listen to them, but I listen. Mama made sure. In the tub under the water, I listened to her. "Judith, you must get clean." Her face was funny through the bubbles. I blew bubbles from the bottom. The tub was full of my voice and Mama's voice, and the light behind her head was like the light behind the Virgin Mary. I cried at Mama's beauty and in my head heard her say, "I indeed have baptized you with water." My tears rose from the bottom of the tub. Her voice was full of prayer. She was so beautiful. Her prayers came down to me along with her eyes and settled on me. Her hands were gentle washing me. Her thumbs held my shoulders in the right way.

One of the men reaches across the aisle and pokes another man in the ribs. The second man's shirt is full of sweat. He slaps the other man. The nurses who are also men tell them to stop. I smell cement. I smell close breath. I grip Nadja's sleeves and tug on her hair.

"I need to leave."

I stand, but Nadja pulls me back down and says, "Judith, you have to sit. Otherwise they'll come and hurt you."

"Why can't I leave?"

"Haven't you been on a bus?"

"I don't like these people."

"Judith. Relax. It's you and me. I'll take care of you."

Their voices are like hot dirt clumping around me. I scratch and dig at the window. The paint is hard. One of my nails snaps back. I yell.

"Judith. You need to stop."

I look at my crooked nail. I bend it and it hurts.

"I need Mama."

"They're going to hit you. Come on and sing a song with me." She begins singing another song I don't know.

"No. Mama will take care of me."

"Shush. Look over there, Judith. There's a man who looks exactly like you."

A little bump of blood comes out of my nail. It looks black. I hold my nail in place and wrap it in the cleanest part of my skirt. The windows push our breath back at us.

"Did you see him?" she says.

"I don't know."

"Look. Over there."

I look over my shoulder and see a man with short hair. His face is red and white. His bottom lip sticks out. His tongue looks dry. He blinks at me, and I turn back and squeeze my broken nail.

"He's nothing like me," I say.

Nadja tilts her head and keeps singing in her small voice. I bite my lip. I wish I could be calm like her.

MICHAEL

I hold the book open, yet not so far that the spine creaks. The sunlight makes the pages seem spongy. I rub them between my fingers.

I take a drink of water and then come upon a familiar passage: "Thus, one can speak of the hygiene of a nation or, in a narrower sense, of a race or of the entire human race." I then skim down a little ways: "This appears to me, if anything, more justified than – as I believe – the hygiene of the entire genus being brought together," and then toward the bottom, "Advancement of this cultivated race is the equivalent of the progress of the entire human race."

I tap the page and close the book. I met the author, Alfred Ploetz, once, shortly before I graduated. He'd come to lecture at the university; the subject was eugenics and its applicability across the medical sciences. Several Party members attended, including the university rector. After the lecture, I approached Ploetz. I meant to question him about what I considered to be his dubious connections between eugenics and psychiatry. I found his ideas much too broad and wanted to say that while I agreed that humanity's advancement depended on our ability to solve our genetic errors, psychiatry, my chosen field, was a science of individual rather than mass solutions, of imaginative engagement rather than physical. In that way, psychiatry was an art. He was standing in a corner of the lecture room, holding a glass of wine and chatting with Eugen Fischer, the rector. I stayed close to the wall, listening for an appropriate time to step in. I reached into my pocket and touched my Party membership pin, acquired the previous week. I listened to them talk and laugh. I debated putting my pin on my lapel. I waited for several minutes. Ploetz looked at me. His eyes were stiff and blue. I looked at the floor. Fischer turned and said, "Ah, Würfel." He waved me over. I stepped forward. My head felt light.

"Alfred, this is Michael Würfel, one of our best students in the psychiatry department."

I shook Ploetz's hand. It was warm and sticky.

"Do you have a question for me?" he said. "You've been standing against the wall for fifteen minutes."

Fischer chuckled.

"No," I said, wiping my temple. "I just wanted to meet you."

"Are you a Party member?"

"Yes, sir."

I pulled out my pin and showed him. He nodded.

"Why aren't you wearing it?"

"I'm sorry, sir. I joined just last week. I'm still getting used to it."

I put the pin on my coat lapel. Ploetz watched me and drank his wine.

"Psychiatry." His white eyebrows cocked a little. "Enjoy that?"

"Yes, sir."

He huffed. "An overcomplicated science. Hardly a science at all, really. Masturbatory in nature. Nothing's quantifiable, nothing's conclusive. Too much is left to interpretation; there's no room for certainty."

"Mm." Fischer nodded. "It is a difficult field."

"Certainty's not everything," I said. "Uncertainty makes things exciting, doesn't it?"

Ploetz frowned. Fischer cleared his throat and glanced at the rest of the lecture room. A number of people looked at me.

"The new Germany," Ploetz said, "is a place of certainty. Of incontrovertible logic. Logic and courage. Germany is undertaking things that other nations have only dreamed of. Britain, America...Germany is setting the example that these nations will want to emulate."

"Not to mention the rest of the world," Fischer said, raising his glass. "It's important you understand that, Würfel, especially if you're wearing that pin."

"Yes, sir."

Ploetz raised his eyebrows at me, then finished his wine and walked away.

I put the book back on the shelf above my desk. The books, most of which address eugenics and racial hygiene, appear to stiffen and age. I move away from the desk and pull my chair over to the window. The smoke looks like a coffee spill in the sky. I glance down the hill toward Hadamar. I can see part of the old bridge; two men and a woman walk across it. A short ways from the institution, a man walks with his dog. He glances up at the sky and pulls his coat tighter around him and hustles forward, pulling the dog after him. I search the yards of a few houses surrounding the clinic. Many of them have outdoor clotheslines, but none have clothing hanging on them.

Some grey residue has accumulated on the window. I scratch it off. The previous day, a woman came in complaining that she had hung her family's clothes on the line and that the ashes from the smoke had dropped onto them. "I hate that I have to wash them again," she said, "and now that it's spring, I want to be able to dry them outside. Can't you please stop that smoke?" A week before that, two children opened the front door and peered inside. Pauline, one of the older nurses, asked them what they were doing, and they ran away. "They looked too frightened to answer," Pauline said. "I imagine that someone dared them."

These sorts of incidents are becoming too common. Our work is quickly becoming the worst-kept secret in Germany, and our lack of security exacerbates the situation. Apparently German mothers have taken to scaring their children by telling them that if they don't behave, they'll be collected by the busses; the mothers call them "murder boxes." On top of that, anyone can – and has – come into the clinic complaining or demanding information. The worst was a woman who came in with her two children. A bus would be arriving in twenty minutes, and she came in carrying an urn. Irmgard, Isabella, and I saw her and told her to visit the administration building across the grounds. She held up the urn.

"I was told these were my husband's ashes," she said.

"We're very sorry," I said.

"I was told he died of heart failure. My family, my children and I went to the river to put his ashes in there."

The two children peered around the room. They huddled close to their mother.

"Frau," Isabella said, "I'm very sorry, but I have to ask you and your little ones to leave. This is a mental institution and no place for a child."

The woman was small but stern. She pointed at the urn's lid.

"I had started to dump these into the water," she said, "when this fell out."

She reached into her pocket and pulled out what looked like a pearl earring. It had been badly scorched, but the hook remained. The three of us looked at each other.

The woman's hand quivered. "Can you imagine my embarrassment?" she said. "Can you imagine the shock?" She shook her head. One of her children began crying. The woman touched the child on her head. She looked at me. "You're the doctor?"

"I'm one of the doctors."

"Are you Doctor Berger?"

"No, I'm Doctor Würfel."

"Where is Doctor Berger? He signed my husband's death certificate."

She took out a piece of paper and showed it to me. It bore the institution's familiar stamp: an eagle straddling a swastika and underlined by the words Hadamar/Mönchberg. I recognized my handwriting across the bottom.

"Doctor Berger's unavailable," I said.

She gave me the urn and said, "Tell me where my husband really is. Tell me whose ashes those are. Do they belong to anyone?" The weight of the ashes surprised me. The three of us were unable to answer. Then Doctor Berner, the head of the clinic, approached us.

"Frau," he said, "I'm sorry, but I need all my staff members right now."

"Are you Doctor Berger?"

"No. I'm afraid none of us have time for you right now. If you have an inquiry, you need to visit the administration building."

"I want to know where my husband is. I want you to tell me right now."

"I really can't say. We deal with hundreds of transfers here. Your husband could be at another institution."

"I was directed here."

"Frau, you and your children need to leave."

"My children deserve an answer."

"And you'll get it from the administration building."

Doctor Berner and Irmgard took the woman by the arm and began leading her outside. The woman resisted, and they had to almost carry her out. When she reached the door, she threw the earring on the floor and thrashed and sobbed, and her children stepped on Doctor Berner's feet. A short time later, the bus arrived. After we finished the intake and escorted the patients into the basement, Benedikt and Ernst took the patients' clothes to administration, where the woman and her children still were. Eventually Doctor Berner called the police, and they removed the family from the hospital grounds. I took the urn downstairs and gave it to Ewald, who put the ashes back in the oven. Irmgard threw away the earring.

I hunch forward in my chair. My palms are wet. I wipe them on my trousers and reach for my glass and finish my water.

SEBASTIAN

There are forty-one patients on this bus, including myself. It's odd that we're being transferred. The Scheuern clinic was hardly overcrowded, and if they badly needed the room, they'd have emptied all the wards, not just ours.

Frederick peers back at me and nods at the nurses. They ignore him. He's discredited himself with his stories: competing in the Berlin Olympics, punching his mathematics teacher in front of the whole class, seducing his mother's friend when he was fourteen, burning a Jewish synagogue last year. Some of the other patients might've been inclined to believe him had I not intervened. Many of them are gullible, if not totally stupid.

I do believe one thing about Frederick, though. A few days ago, as he walked past my bed, he stopped and told me that when he was seventeen, he'd seized his family's cat, Hermes, and carried him into the kitchen and thrown him in the oven. "He just screamed," Frederick said. "The oven just rattled. He jumped and ran around and around and just went wild, and he didn't stop screaming. And he smelled. Smelled like burning cat spit. Think about that."

I'm not sure if I believe the story, but I believe he'd do such a thing. He's threatened a few patients, including me, and he tried to escape Scheuern a few times, once by hitting a nurse over the head with a chair, and each time he was beaten and sedated. Now he thinks that he can prove his worth by policing the rest of us. Nobody here believes him, and I'm grateful for that, but when we arrive in Hadamar, I'll have to convince the new patients.

Emmerich's widened the tear in the seat in front of us. He spreads it using his thumb and forefinger and sticks his fist inside and pulls out a few tufts of stuffing. He holds them up. I nod. Thomas is still sedated. His head lifts whenever the bus hits a bump. I watch him for several minutes. He makes little noises; I think he's dreaming. He's been sedated so many times that the Nazis have probably left an imprint on his mind, to which he returns whenever he's injected.

Emmerich nudges me. "Can you tell a story?"

"No."

"Please."

I shake my head. Stories no longer help me fight off my compulsion, so telling them seems futile. The last few weeks, I've had to listen to the stories of the other men on the ward: Peter, Leopold, Frederick, and the others. They can't help but tell. Their stories are all they have. Of all their tales, Peter's is the oddest, Leopold's is the saddest, and Frederick's is the falsest. Telling seems to provide them with little comfort. Whenever I told a story – usually a Grimm's tale – I did so half-heartedly. I never told them my own.

Up ahead, Peter and Leopold talk quietly. Peter shakes his head. Leopold rubs his temples. Like me, Peter really shouldn't be here. If his story's true, he's a victim of his own momentary stupidity. He'd been drafted for the war but didn't want to fight, so to prevent desertion charges, he went to the local market and stripped himself naked and picked up a potato and began wiping his rear end with it. When he was sent to be mentally evaluated, he tore up a few pages of the doctor's notes and swallowed them. He then tried to draw a penis on the doctor's forehead. He escaped the war but was institutionalized, leaving behind his wife and son. Shortly after being committed, he was sterilized and transferred to Scheuern, away from his home just outside Munich.

There's a cowlick just above Thomas' temple. I want to wet my thumb and smooth it out.

NADJA

The bus rattles. Somehow the rattling makes me thirsty. The air hulks around us. Someone's farted. Maybe several people. Once one starts, the others take it as permission, no matter what it is: farting, screaming, laughing, crying, fighting. A few masturbated at night-time. The blankets moved. It all started with one.

The nurses stare back at us all. They fold their arms. The curtain behind them sways, but I can't see anything past it.

Judith sucks on her broken nail and whispers to her mother. Her words stumble around her finger. I titter. She hits me.

"Shut up."

"Sorry."

"Shut up, Nadja."

"The way you talk." I put my finger in my mouth. "You sound like an ape. Gawaaagwuggawaaag."

I let her hit me. I make a fist with my bloodied hand and sit on top of it. Then, with her finger still in her mouth, Judith cowers away toward the window and resumes whispering to her mother. The nurses and most of the other women on the ward think she's schizophrenic, but they haven't spent enough time with her. As with most of us, Judith's diagnosis was expeditious. The Nazis don't realize that when she talks to her mother, she's actually talking to her conscience, and what's so brilliantly terrible and funny about it is that her conscience seems smarter and more articulate than she is. It looks like she's talking to someone else, but she's absorbed so much of what her mother's said to her that she's retained her mother's manners and rhetoric. It's basically acting. Even her voice changes from moment to moment. And I imagine she says her mother's name because it comforts her. She's still an idiot, after all.

She begins reciting Matthew seventeen-fifteen. She's recited it many times. The devil apparently lived inside a lunatic child, and Christ's disciples couldn't heal him, so Christ appeared and healed the child simply because he believed and the disciples didn't. Raphael painted the scene in *The Transfiguration*. The child's eyes twisted in two different directions. Christ hovered over everyone, majestic and brilliant and, in his majesty and brilliance, self-righteous. He didn't look at anyone; he just stared straight ahead, like a narcissist thoroughly conscious of being admired. Yes, yes, thank you, thank you.

Sometimes Judith's piousness galls me. I laugh in spite. If there is a God, I doubt he'd listen to an idiot. I doubt he'd listen to any of us on this bus.

LEOPOLD

I feel bigger. It's the constriction of the bus. My elbows and legs bloat outwards, and I nudge Peter by accident. I look up. He stares at the curtain. The curtain sways. As though something or someone is about to burst forth.

This bus is a blindfold. All the brightness lies at the front. The dim light shifts on the ceiling – heat stretches through the painted windows. It's impossible to orient.

I wipe the sweat from my forehead. My clothes have tightened. I close my eyes and listen for something constant and regular so as to diminish everything else. The bus slows then speeds up again – the fluid in my head recedes and then rolls forward. My head absorbs the heat. I tip it side to side – the fluid swishes. I picture my brain in a bathtub struggling for air. My battered tongue hovers dryly between my teeth. Behind me, two women talk. Their voices sound like dumping gravel in a puddle.

Peter's arm touches my leg. His eyes flat as soiled cloth. He licks his beard. I push his arm away. It falls back against me. I push it away. It falls back.

"Peter."

He says nothing. His eyes don't move. I shake his arm.

"Peter."

He licks his beard again. One of the women behind me says in a thick voice, "That's why Jesus saved the child." The other woman says, "Yes, and left the rest of us all alone here. That arrogant prick."

The woman's cries sound like hiccups. Peter folds his lip into his beard. He lifts both his hands into his lap.

"You know what they're going to do to us?" he says.

I look over at the nurses. Two of them drink from a flask, awakening my thirst. I swallow. The scars on my tongue blush up. Peter tilts his head toward me. His eyebrows hook.

"A fitting end to my pathetic story," he says. "After everything that's happened, they finally kill me, with a bus full of people nobody wants. It's almost harmonious."

His breath scratches through his teeth – a chuckle. I shut my eyes. My heartbeat's like a toad's throat in my head.

FREDERICK

They stand on a balcony, just him and the Führer. *The* Führer *beckons him. In the uniform of the* Schutzstaffel, *Frederick's shoulders are wide and square. He spent over an hour polishing his boots and twenty minutes tamping down his hair. It is sunny in Berlin. Below the balcony, a crowd of ten thousand people watches him. When he glances sideways, they smile at him. Someone in the crowd shouts, Germany is proud! and many others cheer. He stands before the* Führer *and salutes. People in the crowd salute with him. The* Führer's *uniform is immaculate. He smells like fresh ironing. He extends his hand. His grip is full and strong. Frederick. Yes, my* Führer. *Thank you for everything you've done. You've made a great contribution to this country. I would do it again, my* Führer. *How many people did you kill? Too many to count, my* Führer. *The* Führer *nods. His blue eyes lift. Some things must be done, no matter how difficult or unpleasant. Yes, my* Führer. *The* Führer *takes a medal and pins it on him. Now, Frederick, I want you to work closely with me. Together, you and I will make Germany the envy of the world. An example for all humanity to follow. Yes, my* Führer. *They shake hands again. The crowd cheers. Some of them chant his name. Frederick sighs. The* Führer *squeezes his shoulder. I know strong men, Frederick, he says. I know how they behave and how they look. And from top to bottom, you are strong. And you will survive.* Blood and honour. The orderlies drink from a flask. I watch them. Short drinks for conservation. I stand and say "Can I have a drink?" He says "You can wait." I say "I've been helping. I'm thirsty." "You can wait with everyone else." The queers scratch the window with their witches' nails. I slap one of them and say "Stop that." They shrink away. Across the aisle Leopold drops his head forward on the seat and covers it with both hands. A soft glint through his thin hair. A jut at the back of his head. I want to pick up his head and crush it. Drop it on the edge of a stair. Blood and honour. Two women sit behind Leopold and Peter. One of them a moron. A face like someone squeezed it into shape. Slanting eyes. Flat nose. The other small and thin. The moron cries. I say "Be quiet. You're going to make everyone else cry." The small one says "Go screw yourself." A few people laugh. I say "Shut up. Shut her up." She says "Shut up be quiet shut up. You sound like one of the *Schweinstaffel*." I say "*Schweinstaffel*?" She says "All your despotic jabbering. Yuh-yubble-luppel-leh." More people laugh. I say "Don't laugh at me." She says "Yubble-luppel-luppel-lorf" and people laugh. I say "I could be from the SS. You don't know." She says "Oh my god that's hilarious." She dips her head. The middle of her hair is white. The moron's stopped crying. I say "You want to get beaten? I'll beat you both." Blood and honour. The moron looks at her. She says "Nadja stop." The small one Nadja's face is red. She says "Jesus Christ. Is everybody listening to this maniac? Like the *Schweinstaffel* would ever accept an asshole like him. Somebody give me a pie. I'll throw it at him." People laugh in soundless huffs. I step into the aisle raising my fist saying "You little bitch." A hand drops on my shoulder. An orderly says "Sit down." He walks over to the women. I sit. The moron hides her face in her skirt. Nadja says "Given his proclivity for violence maybe he does work for the *Schweinstaffel*. Not much difference between them and us is there?" The orderly says "That's enough. Both of you shut up. You're upsetting the other patients." Nadja says "They're just laughing. There's no harm." The orderly says "Shut up" and turns away. Nadja sticks her tongue out at him. People giggle. I say "Shut up!" The orderly turns and slaps Nadja in the face. The moron ducks down. Nadja holds her nose and says "You fucking dick. We're not allowed even a little bit of joy. Even our laughter has to be regulated. Fucking cretin."

The orderly slaps her again. "Fucking asshole dickhead troglodyte. You go to school to learn how to do that?" The orderly says "Get a syringe." One of the others comes with a needle. They move the moron and wrestle Nadja still. She shouts "You fucking Jesus fascists. You cock-sucking pigs." They inject her. They put the moron back and say "If you start crying again we'll do the same to you." She shuts herself behind her skirt. They return to the front. One says "They're all a bunch of fucking children." Blood and honour. We want this party to be hard not soft and you must steel yourselves for it in your youth. I say "Hey I'm not a child." They sit back down and take another drink from the flask. I say "I'm not like them. I was going to stop her." One of them says "Good for you." I say "Can I have a drink?" "No." "Why not?" "Be quiet." "I'm helping you. I'm a man. I'm not an idiot." "Be quiet." "I'm a man. Goddamn it." It is not the state that orders us but it is we who order the state.

NADJA

I inhale slowly and close my eyes, which are full to the hilt with tears. Judith hunches over me.

"Can you get up?" she says.

She tugs at my arm. I struggle against the collapse of sedation, the soft dip into myself. I mumble something about being a criminal and that if laughter is a crime, I don't want to live.

A few minutes pass. The heat of the bus and the pain in my nose drain away. Everything loosens and cools. Judith hauls on my arm. She puts her hand under my neck and pulls me and sits me upright. I breathe slowly. Sedation is a lonely state. At the same time, there's no pressure. Judith shakes my arm. My sweet, simple sentinel.

I stare ahead. In the marshy light, the nurse who injected me looks like *Scharführer* Kammer. The same gaze that relies on surface rather than substance. The same brusque and humourless manner. I blink; the illusion persists. Perhaps there's a high degree of inbreeding amongst the *Schweinstaffel*.

After they picked me up, Kammer's *soldats* put me in a small office. Kammer sat across his desk from me. He gave me a cup of coffee with cream and sugar. I drank it and asked for another. He brought it for me and then reached into his desk and brought out a file and a stack of pages. He whisked through my personal history: my family, my schooling, my time as a vaudevillian, my associations with different actors. At one point he glanced at me and frowned.

"You look bored," he said.

"I've long assumed the *Schweinstaffel* have kept a – "

"Don't call us that."

"I've long assumed you've kept a file on me. You're just reading me things I already know."

"Fair enough." Kammer put the file back in his desk. "Your fellow actors aren't nearly so calm. In fact, many of them are quite afraid."

I waved the coffee's steam toward myself and sipped it. Kammer studied me. He asked if I'd ever been mentally evaluated. I smiled a little. My friend Wilhelm had asked me the same question a few days before. He'd said I had a morbid sense of humour. I had told Wilhelm that I was an original, a female Pierrot, and that in modern Germany, anyone who laughs freely is thought to be morbid. "It's stifling," I said, "and it breeds ignorance and complicity." I told him that German laughter is too stiff, too regulated, that our entertainments focus too much on execution and not enough on passion. I said that there was no room in Germany for a Buster Keaton or a Charlie Chaplin or any other comic actor who bites his thumb at authority. "But," I added, "there's still opportunity, especially in the underground. If we're careful, we can work right beneath their noses while getting under their skin. We can galvanize people while making them laugh."

"Frau?"

Kammer cocked his head.

"Is it wrong for me to be calm?" I said.

"It's unusual. Most people, and women in particular, are usually quite anxious."

"I've never had a reason to be mentally evaluated. I'm one of the sanest people you'll meet."

Kammer smiled and touched the pages on his desk. "Are you close with Wilhelm Greiss?"

"We're friends. And we've worked together several times. You know this, I imagine."

"Did you work with him on this script?"

He pushed the pages toward me. I picked them up and saw the title *The Rats* on the front.

"I had some input," I said, "but he did the bulk of the writing."

"Do you know where Greiss is right now?"

"He didn't show up at rehearsals yesterday. I'm guessing he fled the country."

"Did he ever mention wanting to flee the country?"

"Several times."

"Where?"

"He never said."

Kammer made a note. "What, in your mind, was the purpose of this play?"

"To entertain. It's a play."

"That's it? Nothing else?"

I drank my coffee. "I haven't had coffee like this in a long time," I said. "It's delicious."

"You were planning to perform this play at a local pub, true?"

"Most of our regular venues are either closed or unavailable, so we had to choose a different facility."

"What's the name of the pub?"

"I don't know. We didn't get that far in our planning. Today was only the second day of rehearsals."

Kammer leaned back in his chair. "Why did Greiss title the play *The Rats*?"

"Because he hates Gerhardt Hauptmann."

"Who's Gerhardt Hauptmann?"

I snorted and put down my coffee. "You don't go to the theatre very often, do you?"

Kammer cleared his throat.

"Hauptmann's a German playwright," I said. "He wrote a play called *The Rats*, and Greiss stole the title."

"Why does Greiss hate him?"

"He's jealous that Hauptmann received the Nobel Prize. Greiss is a bit of a snob."
"Is Greiss implying that we're rats?"

"Meaning the *Schweinstaff – Schutzstaffel*?"

"National Socialists?"

"I don't see it that way."

"How do you see it?"

"It's comedy. Humans acting as rats, eating other humans."

"That sounds disgusting."

"It plays with expectations. Many of our best-known stories involve death and other morbid things. This play allows us to laugh at those things."

"Why should we laugh at them? Especially now that our nation's at war. Many people would be outraged."

"But that's the point. The play diminishes or deflates all the seriousness and gives us relief. A clown earns louder laughs in wartime than in peacetime."

"Who said that?"

"I did."

Kammer put his pencil down. "So the play implies that we're all rats. Is that it?"

I tilted my head from side to side. "If I explain, then the magic goes out of it. You could view it one way or another. Have you read it?"
"I've skimmed through it."

"Let me recite a scene for you. Then you can judge for yourself. Do you mind?"

Kammer lifted his hand. I flipped through the script and found a scene halfway through.

"Now the action takes place in an old house. The Black Plague's come and gone, and all that's left are the rats, and this family of rats goes into the house and finds a number of dead children. Maria Schwartz, that's my character, goes to a little boy and begins gnawing on his leg. 'Maria!' the father says. He stomps his feet on the floor, stands upright, hands or paws at his sides. 'Observe the proper meal protocol!' And the father takes out a knife, a fork, and a napkin. 'Sorry, father!' Maria says. She giggles and waits as the father and the rest of the family say a prayer for themselves and for all the rats in Germany. Their paws are all put together, the way people pray. Then Maria digs her fork into the boy's leg and begins eating."

Kammer put his hands together. He smiled a little.

"Well," I said, "what do you make of it?"

The bus' noise drains away. My tears correct themselves and slip straight down. I look at Judith and then at the others around the bus. Everyone looks like a spirit. I feel like one. Judith searches my eyes. Hers are full of pleading. I smile at her and lean into my voice and, just before I close my eyes, say, "This is what limbo feels like."

SEBASTIAN

The town rests about half an hour outside of Munich. The library is small but reputable, nestled at the edge of a small wood. On the walls of the front foyer hang paintings by local artists; dozens of children's drawings frame the announcements board. The library's holdings include a collection of Wagner's letters and hand-written scores, and an original copy of *Faust*. Although the number of borrowers has diminished over the last few years thanks to the war and the Party's restrictions on reading material, children still frequently visit, and many of them attend story time. Three times a week, in the late afternoon, I sat in the wide brown chair in the corner of the library and, with a book balanced on my thighs and a cup of tea set carefully on the chair's arm, told stories for an hour. The chair was about a hundred and fifteen years old, and had been repaired and refurbished several times. I took my time sitting down, sinking back and letting the chair surround me. The children sat down before me on the vast blue and green carpet, gazing up at me.

I endeavoured to make the stories as vivid as possible. I practiced them at home the night before, and as I told them, I used different voices for different characters, and I forced a quiver in my throat whenever a climax or terrible event arose. Many times the children asked me to retell certain tales, especially *The Six Swans* and *Hansel and Gretel*. I imagine that having the woods just outside the library made those stories that much more real for them.

For nearly a decade, I sat in that chair and told stories. The children clapped and laughed, hollered and cried, and after three years, the library expanded the sessions to five times a week. I guided the children through fear and dismay into joy and triumph. Some of the stories were dark; I told these in a low voice, leaning forward and inviting the children closer. As time passed, I found that I had a gift for measuring their mood. If they were too excited, I switched to a sombre voice, and if they were shaken by a frightening image, I immediately made a joke. During our time together, we developed intimacy, and that intimacy became a relief.

The bus shudders to·a stop. Many people stand.

"All of you, sit down and stay where you are," says one of the nurses. "It's just a checkpoint. We'll be leaving again in a few minutes."

"Can't we open the windows?" I say. "It's hot and it stinks in here."

"And water," someone says. "What about water?"

I breathe through my mouth. In addition to all the sweat, I'm certain that at least one person has defecated. Two nurses stand and slip past the curtain. I lean into the aisle so I can see. There's a car in front of the bus, and a truck is parked in front of the car. Two SS guards stand in the middle of the road. Both of them hold machine guns. I can't tell where we are.

"What are they doing?" Emmerich says.

"It's nothing," I say.

"I need to pee."

"You have to hold it."

"Can't we go out?"

"Not right now."

"When?"

"There's a ways to go yet."

"How long?"

I shrug. Emmerich pinches his legs together and stomps on the floor with both feet. At the front, the curtain parts and a guard advances. He looks about twenty. He holds his machine gun in front of him and studies us. I look at Thomas. His head is still and just visible above the seat. The guard steps forward. Frederick stares at his gun with the awe of a child. The guard looks at me. His eyes are brown.

He says over his shoulder, "What's wrong with them all?"

A nurse steps forward. "Anxiety, schizophrenia, idiocy, manic-depression, sexual deviancy. An assortment of afflictions."

"Forty-one of them, you say?"

"Forty-one, yes."

The guard looks at Leopold and makes a worried face. He then moves over to Thomas. "Is he sleeping?" he says.

"Sedated."

"Why is he by himself?"

"We thought it'd be best."

"He looks normal. Why is he sedated?"

"Prone to violent fits."

"He's drooling."

"Yes. Morons and such."

"How long ago was he sedated?"

"An hour or two."

The guard nudges Thomas with his gun. He leans forward and lifts Thomas' face, tilting it from one side to the other, his thick fingers pressing into Thomas' white cheeks.

"Just like a regular child," he says.

Thomas opens his eyes; I see his lashes lift. He screams in the guard's face. The guard shouts and leaps backward, bumping against a seat. His machine gun jars and fires, a quick, fierce clatter. Thomas' hair kicks out. Blood pops out the back of his head and onto the women behind him and onto the painted windows. His body seizes and drops back onto the seat. Everyone else on the bus screams and ducks. Emmerich whimpers and pulls on my shirt. The guard looks at his gun and then at the nurses. He stammers and swears. Two more guards enter the bus, whipping the curtain away.

"What happened?"

The young guard looks at Thomas. The other two approach him. They are both older.

"What the hell?"

"It was an accident," a nurse says. "The boy suddenly came awake and surprised him, and the gun went off."

The guards glance around. My mouth is wide open; I've sunk to my knees. I slowly pull myself up, squeezing the seat. A high-pitched sound rattles at the back of my throat. Everyone but Frederick remains ducked down. Frederick looks perplexed. The young guard makes a noise like he's trying to catch his breath. He grabs a seat and steadies himself. Thomas' bare white feet hang over the aisle. I shake. I put both hands on the seat in front of me.

The older guards take hold of the young guard. "Let's go outside. Don't say anything." The young guard's mouth falls open. The older guards guide him to the front and tell him not to worry. He walks with a stiffened gait. They take him outside. I try to step forward, but Emmerich keeps pulling on my shirt. One of the older guards comes back and gathers the nurses close to him. The women hit by Thomas' blood try desperately to wipe it on the seats and, when that fails, on each other. They shout and begin hitting one another. One man looks at Thomas' body and vomits into the aisle. Another man points and says, "Look at the blood. So much blood in that little head." Some people scream for someone to take the body away. The nurses tell them to be quiet. Some of them punch the windows; a few others stumble out of their seats and run for the door. "Let us off! I want to get off!" The nurses shove them back, and the guard aims his machine gun. "All of you shut up! Now! You sit down or I'll shoot you." He pokes a man in the chest with the gun. The man backs away; his leg brushes Thomas' feet, and he gasps. Emmerich squeezes my arm and pulls me down to the seat. I hold my head. My breath comes in dry wisps. The guard says something to the nurses and leaves the bus. Three rows up, blood spreads along the floor.

The guard comes back in again. He speaks to the driver, then to the nurses. He pulls the curtain shut and stands in front of it, holding his machine gun before him. The driver closes the door and puts the bus in gear, and we begin to roll forward. "Is he dead?" Emmerich says.

He squeezes my arm harder. His hand trembles. His eyes are wet and red. I smell urine. Emmerich's pants are damp. I move away a little. Frederick stares at me; his expression is grave. Thomas' bare feet sway above the aisle. A nurse walks up the aisle with his coat and drapes it over him.

"Move him!" a woman cries. "Move him away!"

The nurse goes back to the front.

"Wait!" the woman says. "You're not going to leave him there?"

"It won't be for long," the nurse says.

"You can't leave him there," Frederick says. "He's dead. He's all bloody."

The nurse shrugs. I stammer. I huff. I stand.

"You can't do that," I say. "It's totally undignified. He needs to be taken to his family. He needs to go to a hospital or a morgue."

"We're already going to a hospital. Now sit down."

"Move it away from us!" the woman says.

"There's nowhere to put it," the nurse says.

"Move it up there!" the woman says.

"No. It'll get in our way, and it'll also distract the driver. Now calm down."

I step forward, still shaking. "This is outrageous. You can't leave him alone like that. He'll fall out of his seat."

"Sit back down."

"Sebastian."

Emmerich reaches for me. I step out of his reach and advance toward Thomas' body. The nurse's coat covers his face. Blood has already soaked through it. The blood on the seat shines.

"Oh God," I say. "Oh Jesus. What is the matter with you people?"

I stoop down to lift his legs onto the seat. Someone pushes me from the side.

"Get away!" Frederick says. "He's not yours. He's dead, so leave him alone."

"He should have someone with him," I say. "We can't just put a coat over him."

Frederick shoves me back. I stumble.

"You stole from him," he says. "You're not taking any more. He's not yours."

Behind him the guard comes toward us, raising his gun. "Both of you sit down. Right now."

Thomas' body rocks with the bus' movements.

"You," the guard says. "You sit here."

"What?" Frederick says.

"Hold him in place. Keep him from falling."

"There's blood all over the seat," Frederick says.

The guard points his gun at Frederick. "Do it. And you," he says to me, "go to the back where you were. You have five seconds."

Frederick looks at me. "Jesus Christ." He looks at the guard and moves Thomas' feet away. He then takes the coat and wipes part of the seat. The coat slips off part of Thomas' face: a skein of blood and skin and gristle. Frederick groans. I turn around. The guard begins counting. I return to my seat. Emmerich takes my arm. Frederick sits down beside Thomas, pushing his body away. Both of Frederick's legs protrude into the aisle. I shudder and duck my head down and cry.

LEOPOLD

I push the top of my head against the seat to quiet the pain in my temples. Peter leans on my shoulder and says, "Did you hear what they whispered to each other? 'It doesn't matter. They'll just put him in the oven.'"

His words make a stiff, papery echo in my ears. Like paper being crumpled and tossed away. I do my best not to sob. The gun swings above me. I wish I had bigger hands to cover my head. I hold it between my knees. The floor is good and dull. The bottoms of my trousers sway. They're loose and greasy. I've worn them for days.

"I wonder if I should say something," Peter says. "Just shout it out. Let people know. What would it matter?"

"Be quiet, Peter."

He drums his hands on his lap. He said they're going to kill us. I massage my temples and keep my eyes shut.

One day, when Aunt Minna was sleeping, Uncle Helmut took me outside behind the house. He said he needed company while he prepared a chicken for dinner. I glanced around and asked him if it was a good idea for me to be outside. He said that I should get outside, just for once, and that now was the best time.

I walked slowly. I hadn't been outside in weeks. Uncle Helmut and Aunt Minna's property was surrounded by trees on all sides except the front, but since we'd gone out the back door, it was impossible for their neighbours to see me. It was quite warm for September. The grey sky muted all the colours along with, it seemed, the smells and sounds. It was perfect for me. Uncle Helmut had a small coop with a dozen chickens. He asked me which chicken looked best; I pointed at a fat young hen, and he lifted it out of the coop. "Good choice," he said. He carried the hen by its neck and walked to the old tree stump, in which the axe, browned by blood, was buried. The stump sat just beside a wooden fence, which had a long piece of twine tied to it. He tied the loose end of the twine to the hen's leg and then picked up the axe and held the hen down. "Stand back," he said. I took a few steps back and looked around. My head had warmed, and my thoughts had loosened. I felt comfortable.

With a quick, efficient chop, Uncle Helmut cut off the chicken's head. He let its body go – it made a short dash toward the house, and then the twine tripped it, and it collapsed on the ground. Blood emerged in feeble drops. I looked at the chicken's little head. Uncle Helmut picked it up. He saw me looking at it and offered it to me. I held it in both hands. Its eyes were small, black marbles. The chopped neck bore only a few drops of blood. I held it up to the sun to brighten its comb. I stroked its narrow head between my thumb and forefinger. Its soft wattle swayed. I looked for the faint shadow of my finger through the thin wattle. I opened its little beak and drew its eyes shut. Its tininess was as precious and exhilarating as a jewel.

FREDERICK

Keeps rocking toward me. I keep pushing him away. Sebastian's crying. The idiot keeps talking to him. Sebastian wants to be here. Wants to hold his body and carry it out. A last rite. A final theft. I told him to stop. Maybe that's why the boy wailed every night. Sebastian was stealing his innocence. *Frederick didn't know. If he had, he would've run. He sat under the bridge, as he did every night. He liked the shade and the privacy. There were beetles and caterpillars, and he used rocks and moss and dirt to build small castles for them, and he put the beetles in the castles and watched them crawl out through the windows like Huns after sacking a village. He let the caterpillars climb his arms and groaned and laughed when they left tiny black droppings on his skin.* His little hands. Shreds of skin on the window. One with hairs on it. Bullet hole in the seat. His slow blood keeps coming. Fucking Sebastian won't shut up. I use the coat. Not many dry spots left. Sebastian won't stop crying. I say "Shut up will you?" The idiot Emmerich keeps saying "Sebastian Sebastian Sebastian." Everyone else is quiet but it's a brittle quietness. People want noise. *Frederick sat under the bridge and gathered up the rocks and dirt and moss to build a big castle. There was a small puddle from the previous night's rain, and he used the water to hold everything together. After he finished the first tower, a man approached him. What are you building? the man said. The man had a thick beard and wore a brown cap and brown clothing. I'm making a castle, Frederick said. Do you need some help? the man said. The man's shoes were muddy and his cheeks were sunburnt and his eyes were small and dark. Frederick said nothing. Where are your parents? the man said. Frederick put a pebble on top of the tower. Where's your father? the man said. Frederick shook his head. Is he around? the man said.* The bus hits a bump. His body moves like a sack of blood. The coat slips. His little head rolls. Looks like something's chewed through it. His hair is messy. His ears are small. I put his arm on his chest. The blood follows me. I wad the coat between me and his body. His blood's on my pants and on my hands. I see people watching the guard and the nurses. They watch us. The guard watches me. I wipe my hands on the seat. *The man took off his coat. My name's Til, he said. He shook Frederick's hand. The man's hand was wet. Who are you? Frederick said. I just said I'm Til, the man said. Why are you here? Frederick said. The man squatted down next to the castle. I worked for the engineers during the war, the man said. Have you thought about using a stick to prop up this tower? Once the dirt dries, it'll crumble. You need to mix up some mud and use a stick to hold everything up. He looked up at Frederick from under his cap. Why are you looking at me like that? the man said. Frederick glanced up toward the road. The man stood up. Don't you want my help? I'm a trained engineer, and I'm telling you your castle won't stand up for long. Frederick studied the man's muddy shoes. My father died in the war, he said. He was a soldier? the man said. Frederick nodded. He saw a beetle crawl beside the man's foot. The man saw it too. He lifted his foot. No! Frederick said. He ran over and pushed the man's foot away and picked up the beetle and carried it over to the castle. So do you want my help? the man said. Frederick said nothing. He got on his knees to shelter the beetle from the man. The man chuckled. Not even a war buddy? he said. No? Fine. The man's shadow whisked across the ground. Something hard hit Frederick in the back of the head. Frederick put both hands on his head and moaned. The man spoke to him. Frederick didn't understand much of what he said. He heard the words "failure" and "country" and "ungrateful." Then the man said, I need something. If you won't let me help you, then you need to give me something. I've earned it, goddamn it. The man pulled Frederick into the shade of the bridge and undid Frederick's pants. Frederick's limbs had been loosened by the blow. He couldn't pull them together to run.*

I'll take you, the man said. Stay still. He hit Frederick again. A small goddamn prize, he said. But I'll take you. Shut up. If you yell or scream or make any noise, I'll eat you. I'll bite your nose right off. The man bit his ear and kissed his neck. Frederick cried quietly while the man took him. I put his other arm on his chest so both arms are folded. One of his eyes is open. I close it and wipe the blood off my hands. I look around. Everyone else's faces look like spoiled meat in the bleached light.

NADJA

The unrest. The anxiety. The air is loaded, stuffed to the pores. I can't speak properly. Even though my eyes are closed, I see my body from the ceiling. I float on a brown and grey pool. I could hang my coat on the stink. Everything happens without me. I become part of the bus, easily overlooked.

I'm thirsty. I open my eyes. The light through the windows is the colour of the bottom of a river. My face is warm. I drag my eyes across the aisle. Their faces look ancient. Judith buries her face in my stomach and sobs and speaks in gibberish. Her voice is higher than usual. Anxiety works like helium.

Judith talks to her mother. She lifts my arm around her. The poor, desperate soul. She's too naïve to realize her mother abandoned her. She kept asking the staff when her mother would come pick her up. It seems that, as with many of the other patients, Judith's mother had had enough. She couldn't tolerate Judith anymore. She had put her faith in God to correct Judith, and when it didn't happen, she, instead of accepting Judith, expunged her test of faith. The last time Judith talked to the staff, she went back to her bed and cried, gathering her sheet into her hands and hiding her face. At that moment she was almost normal.

I patted her leg and rubbed her back. I asked her if she wanted to hear a song. She asked me to sing "Amazing Grace." I said, "Let's pick a different song," and I began singing "*Die Gedanken sind frei.*" I rocked Judith back and forth; she smiled, and as I sang, some of the others in the ward watched us. A few came and sat on the bed across the aisle. Even Silke, who'd bitten my hand the day before during a Chaplin impression

– she'd mistaken the moustache for Hitler's – listened quietly, humming along. One or two of the others joined me. Judith began to clap. When we came to my favourite verse – "*Drum will ich auf immer den Sorgen entsagen!*" – the fat troll and her minions approached us and told us to stop, that we were upsetting the other patients. I scoffed and said, "Come on. Look at them. If they were any more upset, they'd be ecstatic." The others smiled. "When am I getting a shot?" I said, holding up my bandaged hand. The troll looked at me and then began to walk away. "Fat *Schweinstaffel* whore," I whispered. She turned and pushed me. Judith stood and shouted. The others looked at the floor. The troll stared at me. I groaned vociferously and fell back on the bed with a flourish, one leg cocked in the air. Judith touched my arm. "See?" I said. "Just a bit of comedy." Judith nodded. The troll grunted and squeezed her lips together and looked at the others. "Worthless bunch," she said. She left the ward. I laughed. So did Judith and the others.

The need for comedy on this bus is overwhelming. If someone doesn't sing or do impressions soon, someone else will get hurt, even killed. A massive fight could break out and not even the guard's machine gun could stop it. I can't lift my limbs or push up my voice. Judith leans into me as into a pillow. She smells like soap. My body follows the bus' movements.

MICHAEL

I tamp my hair down with pomade and, using my mirror, glance around my room and wonder about its dimensions. The shower room in the basement is almost the same size. On the first of April, we packed ninety-one people into it. I helped usher them in, but I didn't remove the oxygen or turn on the carbon monoxide. That was Doctor Berner's job. Once all the patients had removed their coats and piled them just outside the shower room, we told them to face the wider wall. It felt like we were packing a car, strategically arranging bags of clothes or food to maximize the amount of space. I then locked the door and helped the nurses carry the coats upstairs. Halfway up the stairs, I paused to listen. The patients were yelling and pounding on the metal door. Then their voices shot into high, blistering octaves. I turned and went upstairs, my footsteps ringing off the concrete.

A few of the people who work here have memories of being frightened or dishevelled by such people. Doctor Berner likes to tell the story of a woman from his hometown who thought she was the witch from *Hansel and Gretel*. "It was widely known that she hated children," Doctor Berner said, "so I think she seized upon the story to justify her hatred, to give herself what she considered to be a proper persona.

"The woman, whose name was Linda, set about filling her home with candy and cakes. Her windows were frosted with sugar, and her living room was piled with cookies and strudels. She never stopped baking for two weeks. Then one day she opened her door, and everyone in town could smell her delicious baking. But most of the children had been warned about her, and so they stayed away. But one day a boy named Gustav, probably dared by his friends, approached the house and knocked on the door. The door had a candy wreath, and he began to pick from it. Then the door opened, and Linda looked down at him. 'Aha!' she said, and she grabbed him and took him inside. Gustav's friends ran away, and they didn't say anything until that evening, when Gustav's parents called them because they couldn't find him. They contacted the police and they all went to Linda's house and knocked on the door. They noticed that the house's smell had changed; it didn't smell sweet anymore. Linda didn't answer the door. The police broke the door in and went inside. They found Linda seated at her table gnawing on Gustav's cooked leg. The rest of him was either in the oven or hanging on hooks at the back of the house. Linda said to them, 'I finished him off. I'm the better witch.'"

During the last few days, I've begun to think that Doctor Berner fabricated this story. The other staff members who as children were upset by mentally ill people tell much soberer tales, and they always end with, "Now that I've worked with these people, I understand that they had no choice in behaving that way." They've forgiven their tormentors. My experiences with such people have been prosaic. Although they routinely fail evaluations of intelligence and logic, evaluations which in themselves are narrow and flawed, they are endlessly fascinating and creative. They possess their own logic, their own philosophies, and so must be addressed on their own terms. But our task demands efficiency over patience. The war has given the *Führer* the excuse to eliminate these people, so we can't spend any time studying them and getting to know them. They also require the entire world to conform to their logic, a sheer impossibility.

On the first of April, after Doctor Berner had finished operating the shower room, he joined me in the office filling out the death certificates. We sat across from each other. To my right was the window, and I could see the smoke spreading across the sky.

"What are you giving that one?" he said.

"Blood poisoning," I said.

"You're still using the same signature? Doctor Berger?"

"Yes."

"Good."

"And you're Doctor Klein?"

"That's right."

I dipped my pen into the bottle of ink and scrawled the signature at the bottom of the certificate. I had tried to give it its own distinct personality, separate from my own signature; my "B" was wide and looping, and I finished the "r" with an upward flourish.

We wrote in silence. Doctor Berner's posture was upright. Despite his short height, he had a proud bearing.

"Doctor Berner, may I ask you a question?"

"Of course."

He put down his pen and put his enjoined hands on the table.

"When you operate the shower room, how does it feel?"

"Do you mean am I uncomfortable with it?"

I nodded. Doctor Berner sat back. He looked at the certificate in front of him and then at the stack of patient files beside him. Each of the files had been marked on the front with a big red plus sign. He dragged his thumb over the files.

"I admit that I was hesitant. What man wants to feel like a murderer? But when I study these people and read their files and see them suffering and confused in front of me, it makes it easier."

"I see."

"Not to mention that we're furthering progress, too. When you're driving down a road, and there's a car ahead of you that's going very slowly, and there are many cars behind you waiting to go, it makes you impatient, doesn't it? It even angers you if you're delayed long enough. You honk your horn and you yell and curse. It's the same idea here. We're essentially eliminating that slow car, allowing human ingenuity and strength to flourish unimpeded. No hindrances. No obstructions. It's intoxicating."

He smiled a little. "There's something else," he said, "and this is between you and me." He leaned forward. "I have to say that there are also times when I feel exhilarated. I walk into the hallway across from the room, and I hear them fighting, and I watch them for a moment, and when I turn on the gas and listen to them, I feel strong, like a bully. I've never experienced that before."

Doctor Berner made two fists and tapped them on the table. His little smile hardened.

"I realize that may sound horrible," he said. "Does that sound horrible to you?"

"Well," I said, "killing that many people in one stroke – I can see why it'd be powerful."

I adjust my coat and leave my room and walk downstairs to the lobby. A large desk stands at one end, complete with pencils, pens, and paper. Isabella and Irmgard fill syringes with Luminal. Ernst prepares the camera. He turns the knobs on the tripod's legs, fixing it in place. He then lifts the camera and sets it at the top.

"Ernst?"

"Doctor Würfel?"

"Can you please turn the camera so that it faces the wall? I don't want the flash in my eyes."

"Oh yes. Sorry."

Ernst rotates the tripod. Isabella looks at me and smiles. I stroke my moustache. A metallic clank spurts through the floor. Another nurse, Benedikt, comes around the corner.

"Benedikt?"

He approaches me, a tall and husky man.

"Did you check on Ewald?"

"Oh. Not yet."

"Could you, please?"

"Are you concerned?"

"A little. Just a little."

"He's working down there right now. Can't you hear?"

"I know he is. I just want to make sure he's stable. Please."

Benedikt nods and leaves the lobby. Outside the window, the black smoke churns in the sky. Isabella touches my arm.

"Do you need anything?"

My stomach tightens as I inhale. "I'm okay."

"Why don't you go for a walk? You said you wanted to."

"Not right now. I'll go after."

"Why don't you go to your room, then? I'll call you when we're ready."

"I don't want to be alone. I need to be around people right now."

Isabella smiles. "Just because Ewald drinks doesn't mean he won't do his job."

"I know."

"I can't blame him for drinking. He's coping as well as anyone else would. Though I wish he'd improve his hygiene. Trim his beard, wash his face. He's beginning to smell like death."

"Mm." I put my hands in my coat pockets. "Do I look like a doctor?"

I straighten my posture. Isabella chuckles.

"If you saw me in a crowd of people, would you guess that I'm a doctor?"

"I don't know," she says. "Like I said, you're young."

I clear my throat. I smooth out my coat and put my hands back in my pockets. "A lot of the patients, when they first come in, they look at me like I can help them. They don't trust Doctor Berner. There was one patient a few weeks ago, a little girl named Rosamunde who didn't want to move away from the corner. Doctor Berner kept ordering her to do it, and she cowered away from him. She cowered away from Irmgard, too, even when Irmgard offered her a piece of candy. And then I stepped in. She came right into my arms, and she looked at me like she was relieved." I shake my head. "I don't know what to do if something like that happens today."

"Let us handle it. You have more important things to worry about than the patients being difficult."

"But that's the problem. I empathize with their being difficult. I'd be difficult, too."

"But that's their life. It can't be helped. Their lives are miserable. Nobody can relate to them."

"I'm a psychiatrist."

"Okay. So you can study them, but you can't relate to them."

"I think I can."

"They don't have the faculties to help themselves. They can't be helped. Life is just too big for them. They can hardly relate to each other, let alone people like you and me. Many of them are not even aware of their own suffering. What kind of hell is that? So really, what we do here is a charitable act."

I cock my head. Benedikt walks up to us.

"Ewald's fine," he says.

"Is he drunk?"

"No. He's ready."

"What about the urns?"

"He has them."

"Thank you."

Benedikt walks away. Isabella tucks her hair behind her ears.

"I know it's heartbreaking, Doctor Würfel," she says. She pats my arm. "Just think like you're ending their suffering. It's an act of mercy."

She moves away and resumes filling the syringes. I step closer to the window and peer up at the smoke. Is life as big as she makes it out to be? Or is it small and simple? Am I suitable or qualified enough to perform acts of mercy?

EWALD

I shut the oven and wipe my forehead on my sleeve. It's soaked through already. I turn away. The heat follows me down the hall, like a child with her hand in my back pocket.

My footsteps are lonely. I think about removing my shoes and walking quietly on the cement. But then I'd feel as if I was wading. It's best to leave them on.

The oven gurgles like a dragon's stomach. The urns are lined up along the wall. When the oven's open, the yellow flames light them up like lanterns. I once asked Doctor Berner how much the Party spends on urns. "If we buy any more, we might bankrupt the war effort," I said. Doctor Berner smiled. One urn weighs about five pounds. Filled to the top, it weighs about eight or nine. Most bodies don't fill to the top. I can look at a man and guess what he weighs, in flesh and ash.

The bodies are always ruddy. Their eyes are always open. They fight each other and struggle until the last, leaving scratches and bruises. I once had to pry two men apart because they'd tried to choke each other. They'd died with their hands around each other's throats. Some people lose teeth or hair. I sweep them up after removing the bodies.

I continue down the hall and sit down. The narrow stairway is just around the corner. I take a quick look up and pull my flask from beneath my shirt. The metal is warm from the oven. I twist off the cap and drink. The whiskey is warm and full. I hold it in my mouth and look up at the scuffed cement ceiling. The whiskey assumes a sacred essence: Take this cup and drink from it. This is my blood.

I pray for Beate. I pray for her protection, and for Helena's strength in sustaining it. I see them in the attic, the window covered with a blanket, the two of them gathered around a candle, playing a game or telling a story. Beate, nine years old, sits in Helena's lap, her small awkward limbs neatly folded. She will remain simple. Thank God. She and Helena have the same eyes: greyish-blue, beautiful and understanding.

Once, Helena sent me a picture that Beate drew. The censors had already opened the envelope. I sat in the cafeteria and looked at it. Benedikt saw it and said, "What's that?"

"My daughter drew it."

"Oh, that's wonderful. How old is she, three or four?"

"Four," I said.

He nodded, and I put the picture away.

I take another drink and put my flask back inside my shirt. They are trying to eliminate every source of human affliction. They call it a mercy death. When they open the shower room and I see the ruddy bodies, and the open eyes that strained to see God through the choking gas, and the excrement and urine and vomit understandably dropped in the face of such a vile and horrifying death, and I lift their bodies one by one onto the trolley and roll them down the hall and lift them onto the rails and slide them into the oven, I see not only the terror and the injustice but also that it will never be enough. As long as humanity exists, they cannot eliminate affliction. I take comfort from this. It makes it seem more likely Beate will survive, and that the comforting simplicity she provides will endure. But my job will never end. I cannot leave. The smoke that stretches from the chimney and out into the sky is a signal of my suffering, a stained arm reaching toward God.

JUDITH

I pull Nadja's arm around me and try to hide. She's too small. I'm bigger than her. But in a way she's bigger than me. It's in that way I want to hide.

Her stomach is soft. Her arm is light on my back. She's easy to hug. I will stay this way. Both of us together and warm.

"Don't whine, Judith."

"Mama. That boy is dead." My jaw on Nadja's ribs.

"Stop crying."

"I saw his blood. I don't want to open my eyes."

"How do you want people to see you? Stop it. You're not in trouble. Sit up."

With her teeth and tongue, Nadja makes little noises. I hug her harder. One day last year or maybe the year before, Mama took me to a doctor. She told me to sit down and she went with him into a different room and asked him, "When will she improve?" She'd prayed before we'd gone. She had put holy water on my forehead and crossed me carefully. We could only go to the church when there weren't many people there. She said she could hear the Lord's voice then. After the doctor she took my hand, and we walked out together. Her eyes were sad. I asked her to hold my hand tighter.

"I'm not good enough, Mama."

"How does hiding help, Judith? Do you want them to think poorly of you?"

"Where are you? Can you come get me?"

"Judith, stop crying."

"They killed the boy. I don't know what to do. I don't want to see him."

"Judith, you're acting like a child."

"No. No no no, I'm not."

"You're acting stupidly."

I hug Nadja. My tears drop onto her shirt. I smell the warm cloth. I pull her arm further around me. Her arm is thin. I like it. I hold her hand and close my eyes.

"Be merciful unto me, O God, for man would swallow me up. He fighting daily oppresseth me. Mine enemies would daily swallow me up, for they be many that fight against me, O thou most high."

Nadja mumbles with her fresh voice that covers my head. I lower myself to hide.

"Say that again," I say.

"Shut up," Nadja says.

I hug her harder. I try to continue the psalm. I cry. I can't continue.

EMMERICH

I lift my pants so they don't stick to my legs hot and itchy pinned by the seat, lifting them like the days after Klaus took me to see the doctor I kept lifting my pant legs afterwards to keep away the itch, I'm not sure when Klaus' hands whipped like swift grey birds in the dark shaking me awake, like a startled horse my hand reared up from under the blanket and swatted him in the face I wasn't fully awake and didn't mean to I might've meant to punch someone in a dream or maybe I thought he was a thief, he told me don't do that again, he sat on top of me and slapped my cheek his knees digging into my shoulders, now listen he said, he said things are going to change something about someone named Hitler something about a law he used a strange word sterilized that I'd never heard before, the name Hitler had an ugly shape in the dark the word sterilized meant nothing, Hitler said that people like me had to be sterilized, I didn't know what that meant, I turned away I wanted to go back to sleep, look at me Klaus said, he dug his fingers into my eyes and I cried, shut up Emmerich be quiet, when I opened my eyes his words hung like red sprinklings in the dark lighting up his face he said sterilized meant that I wouldn't be able to have children, he made scissors out of his fingers and snipped at the end of my nose I turned my head away he pulled on my jaw and forced me back, look at me and listen or I'll thumb your eye out Mama loves that you'll always be a little child he said so does Papa because you're strong he can ask you to do anything and you'll do it for him, I'm not a little child I said, they think that I'm the difficult child he said they tell me to shut up about you and to get out, I will get out but not before I do something about you I won't let someone like you win their favour over me, as Klaus spoke I thought about children, I'd never thought about having children before

I never thought I could but now he was saying I could and also that I couldn't, the thought made my penis stir, who would I make children with I said, yes nobody would have you anyway he said but I'm going to make sure that you don't have any children if someone's going to give Mama and Papa the gift of grandchildren it'll be me

Sebastian with his red eyes moves over and lifts his legs because of the puddle holds his hand over his nose and mouth I think it's the boy and the smell, I'm sorry I say, I move around lift up from my seat put my finger in the rip in front of me and feel a sharp end like a tooth, I pull my finger over it over it over it pull it out and my finger is dark pink, Sebastian stares forward where the boy was shot he says I can't believe they're just leaving him there, staring forward sad and angry like he could kill someone, I'm hungry and thirsty have a headache, the man with the gun looks at me I look down, Sebastian I say I'm sorry about the boy, Sebastian makes a sound, Sebastian, Emmerich be quiet, did you love that boy, Emmerich please leave me alone, can you say your thoughts please just your voice for me, no be quiet and leave me alone, Sebastian puts his hands on his knees, the itching I want to take off my wet pants

the smell of the first hospital got onto my hands and shoulders, a small woman sat against the wall she had a little girl with her, the girl liked me and looked at me walked up to me and walked back and walked up to me she liked looking up at me, a young boy came out with a doctor and a nurse behind him, the doctor had black hair he asked the small woman to bring her son back the next day, the small woman nodded put her hand on her son's shoulder, the boy looked at my knees he pushed out his lips walked out with his mother and his sister, his sister waved to me then Klaus swatted my leg, I got up the doctor stretched his neck as he looked at me, he had a file in his hand he looked at it as we walked over, hello Emmerich he said and he said his name and the nurse's name and asked us to follow him, they took us down a hallway, Klaus let me go ahead of him, he was treating me much better gave me a pretzel before, how tall are you Emmerich the doctor said, six-foot-seven Klaus said, please let him answer the doctor said, how much do you weigh Emmerich, I looked at Klaus he stared at me I don't know I said, two hundred and forty six pounds Klaus said, extraordinary, the doctor smiled at me and said something about it being a pity that Klaus isn't as big or that size doesn't run in the family, my brother licked his lips and glared at the doctor, we went into a small room the doctor told me to sit down at the little table, he stopped Klaus at the door and told him to wait outside, are you sure Klaus said, the doctor closed the door leaving Klaus outside, the doctor sat down in front of me the nurse sat behind the doctor, why does Klaus have to stay outside I said, I'm scared when I'm around Klaus but being with the doctor and nurse was a different kind of scared, those are the rules the doctor said only you need to be in the room, he opened his file and picked up a pencil, he said he was going to ask me some questions, I was afraid and asked for Klaus to come in the doctor said no then asked me a question about something that happened in Germany in a certain year I can't remember which one, I remember saying that Mama had baked a cake for me and that Mr. Schaffer's horse had died and that her name was Jewel and that Klaus had gone to Berlin, the doctor asked why Klaus went to Berlin, I said he'd gone with his friends and I didn't know why they went, that's fine the doctor said now I'm going to ask you a math question, I straightened, the doctor asked me to divide a big number by a small number I think it was seventy-two and nine, I groaned Mama had tried to teach me math by using corn kernels the highest I went was what is twelve plus eight which is twenty, we didn't have enough kernels on the table she never taught me how to divide, so I thought of the bigger number seventy-two and nine was the smaller number which meant the answer had to be less than seventy-two but bigger than nine, I knew that nine was an odd number and seventy-two was even which meant the answer had to be odd because two odd numbers make an even number like how five and seven are twelve and five and three are eight, I said twenty-seven or maybe seventeen, the doctor wrote my answer down, is that right I said, not quite he said, what's the answer then, never mind about that Emmerich let's try another question, the doctor read the file, my seat felt small, I looked at the door I wanted Klaus in the room so he could answer for me

the bus stops then goes again, I hear the boy's feet drop, his blood like an accident on the windows, Frederick moves him around watching for the blood, come on this is fucked up Frederick says can't you move him away, toss him out the door someone says he's stinking up the whole bus, Sebastian makes a sound, it's not the boy Frederick says it's all of you useless mongrels, Sebastian leans into the aisle like he's going to leave I pull on his arm to stay and talk his voice is soft, did you love that boy I say, Emmerich he says coughing and crying oh Jesus oh Jesus

don't tell Mama and Papa Klaus said if you do I'm going to put a knife in your back do you understand, now just do this for me think of this as serving Germany you wouldn't be able to go to war but you can do this for Germany it's for the greater good Emmerich, Klaus patted me on the shoulder, the doctor and the nurse took me into the back, the doctor told me to sit down asked me to take off my clothes put on a robe sit on a bed, I didn't like the floor in the room it looked dirty and there were lots of black marks like they were made with a poker, I had to wait a long time before another doctor came in he and the first doctor told me to lie down they took me into a bigger room put a mask on my face I wanted Klaus in the room I meant to say that but the mask stopped me I fell asleep, I awoke with pain in my testicles reached down and felt them big and stinging, Klaus was there he said you can't help Papa for a while we'll tell him you injured yourself okay I'll explain everything to him and Mama okay, Klaus' proud eyes I gave him my hand he squeezed it, I squeeze my pants that same itch

FREDERICK

I take an arm of the coat and cover his head. His salty smell thickens what's already in the air. The bus slows and speeds up. He almost slips off the seat. I hold him and prop him up as best as I can. Many times I've seen myself as a bullet burrowing into a man's chest man's head man's stomach and feeling the warm ecstasy of finality. The fibres giving way before me. Nestling into the warmth which is welcoming and peaceful. The poor useless boy. There wasn't much for him and what little there was Sebastian stole. Sebastian won't stop crying. Like his toy's broken. Like his dog's died. When he finds another boy he'll forget Thomas. I'll keep watching him. Men like me win wars. Men with my resolve. My steady hands. My tight shoulders. We stride into the jagged areas where the bullets shred the air. We kill the right way. With finality. If the *Führer* wants to win he should liberate me from this den of idiots. They squawk. All of them useless. Step on them. Eliminate them. Vaporize them. The soldier's straight gun glinting hard. Peter stands. His eyes slick with nothing. He says something about an oven. The guard hits him with the butt of his rifle. He falls back. At the dull sound the smell of blood grows fuller. *Mama's hands were covered with blood and fat. Frederick. What, Mama? I want you to go to Borlitz's. She wiped her hands on her apron. Hermes mewed and curled around her leg. I'm busy, Mama. You're not doing anything. Go down quickly and buy half a dozen eggs. I need them for the batter. I was going to the river. You can go tomorrow. Now you're wasting time. If this chicken goes bad, we'll have nothing to eat.* Leopold moves away. The guard beats Peter telling him to shut up. Leopold's head like a brontosaurus egg grinding his teeth in the night and biting through the sheet to his tongue. His hands flapping back. And in the daytime bitching about his aunt. All of them with problems and no will to force them out. No goddamn will. *Frederick walked down the dirt road and turned up the stone path toward Borlitz's market, taking the long way around the bridge. There were very few people. It was a Tuesday afternoon, and most people were at work or at home preparing for dinner. He took his time, walking around each tree and kicking each rock. He fingered the money in his pocket. A short ways from the market, there was an old fountain. Frederick curled around a tree and walked over to it. There were no coins at the bottom. He took the money from his pocket and, one by one, flicked the coins into the water. Two men passed him. One of them said, What do you think you're doing? Do your parents know you're wasting money like that? It's my money, Frederick said. Let's walk away, the other man said. Why? That's the Hesse boy. The first man's face slackened. The men left. Frederick took the last coin and threw it down into the water.* Sebastian with his chair in the corner of the ward distracting everyone with his stories. *The Wolf and the Seven Children. Jorinda and Joringel. The Twelve Brothers.* But everyone knows about his dreams. Can't hide them. His body lifting off the bed disgusting rising to meet whatever boy it was. "Robert" and "Hans" and the rest. Every morning he took his sheets off the bed. His face stiff to hide the shame. *What is wrong with you, Frederick? Mama hung her head and put her hands up to her face. I don't understand why you behave this way. It's not natural. You don't listen to me, Frederick said. I listen to you all the time, Mama said. You always say you have plans or that you're doing something important. Frederick stiffened. What are you doing? his mother said. You're not helping me around the house. You're not working. From what I can see, all you do is walk around with your hands in your pockets. Frederick leaned against the wall. I think about things, he said. What things? Things I want to do. Ambitions? Sort of. What does that mean? I look forward to doing them. I'm just building my abilities in my head, working up to them. Mama shook her head. It's laziness. Uselessness. You're even more useless than your father was. Frederick made fists. Not useless, he said. Only a useless man would die of a stroke two miles behind the front line. Mama shook her head. Forget it. I want you to go back to the fountain and get the money, she said. The chicken's ruined, so buy some bread. Go now. Frederick huffed through his teeth. Are you going? Mama said. Oh for the love of God. She turned off the oven and left the kitchen, muttering to herself. The chicken's dressed corpse remained on the counter. Frederick approached it. A commotion of blood and feathers framed the cutting board. The chicken yawned open at the stomach. Its ribs looked like the trellises on the gate at Frederick's old school. It smelled infected. Mama had washed the cleaver and put away the basin. Frederick picked up the cleaver, studied it, then put it down. Hermes approached him and rubbed against his leg. His fur was grey; his eyes were greenish-yellow. Frederick watched him for a moment. He bent down and picked Hermes up. Frederick nudged his nose against Hermes'. He moved to the oven and opened it.* The guard hits Peter again. Peter's face dark and bloody. The light on the walls and ceiling like rotten teeth. People cry. They bury their heads.

LEOPOLD

My heart croaks in my head. My heartbeat's red against the backs of my eyes. I see the red outline of my teeth. I cradle the bus' heat on my tongue. Everyone's breath squats on the back of my head. I lick my lips. My teeth clamp down on an old scar. I have a child's teeth. My little jaw a loose appendage of my bulbous head. The idea of death is like coming home after years away.

I feel the seizure just before it arrives, like the ground vibrations of an arriving train. My jaw and neck pump together. My dry tongue's trapped. I desperately wish for water. A charge hooks up my spine – my spine hooks. My head jams against the seat. My shoulders bunch. My hands flail. I hit Peter on the knee. He's knocked out. My little teeth dig past the scar tissue. Blood rises to my mouth's ceiling. I lift my lips at the corner. I try to aim for a small untouched portion of my tongue, lest I bite all the way through it. The bright scar tissue gives way. I hum and curl toward the wall. The smell is overwhelming. My back is hot. Everyone's voices drip down the walls onto my back. The bus is a can of sloppy voices.

MICHAEL

When I was about six years old, my father told me a story called *Godfather Death*. In it, a poor man has twelve children, and when he has a thirteenth child, he decides to find help and so seeks a godfather for his newborn son. Three volunteers step forth: God, Satan, and Death. God says, "I will take charge of the child and make him happy." But the father refuses God because He takes from the poor, gives to the rich, and is concerned only with the afterlife. Then Satan comes forth and says, "I will give your child gold, and he shall never want for anything." But the father refuses Satan, for obvious reasons. Then Death steps forward. "I am Death," he says, "and I make everything equal. I will provide for your son." So Death becomes the boy's godfather.

Years later, when the boy comes of age, Death meets him and takes him into a forest, and shows him a rare and sacred herb. "This is my gift to you," Death says. "You will become a famous physician. When you are called to a patient, I will appear to you. If I stand near the patient's head, you can say with absolute certainty that you will heal him, and then give him this herb so he can recover. But if I stand near the patient's feet, you cannot help him. You must give him to me. If you try to deceive me, you will be punished." Within a short time, the young man becomes the most celebrated physician in the world, blessed with the uncanny ability to glance at his patient and immediately say whether he will live or die. People from all over the world consult him, and as a result, he quickly becomes wealthy.

One day a messenger calls for the physician. "The king is sick! The king is ill!" The physician goes to the king and, upon entering his chamber, finds Death standing at the foot of the king's bed. The king pleads with the young doctor to save him. The doctor considers for a moment; the king is a wise and beloved ruler, and his death will outrage his subjects. The doctor decides to take a risk: he stoops and turns the king around so that Death stands at his head. He then gives the king the sacred herb, restoring him to perfect health.

Death is furious. "You've deceived me," he says. "This time I'll overlook it, because you are my godson. But if you do that again, I will take you with me."

Within a short time, the messenger appears again. "It's the king's daughter! She's dying!" The physician returns to the castle and finds the king's daughter on the bed. At the foot of her bed stands Death. "Help her," the king pleads. "If you help her, the two of you may marry." Despite her cold pallor, the princess is very beautiful. The physician looks at Death and again decides to deceive him. Once he turns her around, he gives her the herb, and she quickly becomes healthy. But Death strides forward and takes the physician by the hand. "Life is over for you," he says. "You will come in her place."

Death leads the physician into a cave deep in the earth. Thousands of candles illuminate the cave. Some of them are tall, some are medium, and some are short. Every second several of them go out, and several are lighted. "Those are children," Death says, pointing to the tall candles. "Those medium ones are adults in the middle of their lives, and those short ones are old people."

"Show me my candle," the physician says, expecting a tall candle.

Death shows him a waned candle bearing a wilting flame. Horrified, the physician begs Death to light a new one for him.

"I cannot," Death says, "for one must go out before I can light a new one."

"Then light the new one with the old one," the physician says.

"Then it will keep burning."

Death picks up a new candle and moves like he means to fulfill his godson's wish. But Death makes everything equal, and so he deliberately drops the worn candle on the floor, snuffing it out, and the physician falls, dead.

When I became a Party member, I resolved to do my duties while preserving the inquisitive, imaginative part of myself. I agreed to maintain secrecy under threat of death. As I swore my oath to the Party, I felt I was taking a sacred vow. The office in which I stood assumed the depth of a chapel. The red and black posters on the walls assumed the solemn brilliance of stained glass windows. I'd been told by professors and fellow students that it was a fantastic opportunity to further my career. "You'll be set for life," they said. "The Party will give you what you need. The research possibilities will be limitless."

But the only things I've learned concern death. Death does not make everything equal; it indicates a person's value, or lack thereof. Death is an instrument of defective judgement. The clenched, pink faces of nearly twenty-nine-hundred people attest to that. Most of all, death ruins memories. When he told the story, my father sat me on his lap and spoke in a slow, soothing voice; we sank into the sofa while a great fire burned in front of us. My experiences have dulled this memory. Also, even though most of us can't control how we're remembered after death, dying amidst strangers, and in such a terrible manner, virtually ensures that each of those people will be pitied, if they're remembered at all.

I can't sit still. I can't stand. I walk around the lobby, trying to smile and appear at ease. It's as though I'm about to enter

Death's cave and walk amongst thousands of candles, all of which are diminished and waiting for me to snuff them. None of them will light up. There will be no new life.

Another metallic clank rises through the floor. I can feel the gas valve in my hand. I know the procedure well, having been shown countless times: once the doors are completely sealed, I remove the air from the room. That's the worst part. With no oxygen supply, the patients' voices quickly lift into unnaturally high registers that leave me nauseated. They screech. They struggle and claw at each other. They climb over one another, trying to find an oxygen source. I once asked Doctor Berner why he waits to turn on the gas; he said because it takes time for the oxygen to clear the room. He stood at the window in the door, watching the patients with an expression of mild absorption, like a child watching a jar full of insects. I'm not sure I believe him now.

Once enough time has passed, I turn on the carbon monoxide. The gas fills the room, obscuring the patients. The patients drum on the door. In their outrage, some of them tear at their fellows; it's not uncommon to find blood on the floor. It takes several minutes for the gas to work, sometimes fifteen or twenty. Some patients possess remarkable endurance. Today, with about forty patients, the gassing shouldn't take more than ten minutes.

I sit in the corner and then stand up and resume walking. Irmgard and Benedikt watch me. Isabella asks me if I want a coffee. I shake my head. My mouth is dry.

SEBASTIAN

I stare at the nurses and the guard. They talk to each other. I wipe my eyes and my nose. I grunt and shove Emmerich's hand off and stand up.

"What is this?" I say. "How can you stand there as if a child hasn't been murdered?" I point at Thomas. "This is murder."

A nurse steps forward. "Sit back down."

"No. Stop the bus. Stop the bus and let us off."

The guard comes forward and raises his gun to my chest. He is sweaty. He grimaces at the smell. Emmerich whines behind me.

"You're going to kill me? You're going to kill all of us?"

"I will shoot you if you don't sit down."

"We're not prisoners. You can't treat us like this. This bus is an abomination. We haven't been given water or food. We can hardly breathe in here. It's like a coffin."

"Five seconds. One."

"Sebastian," Emmerich says. "Come back."

"I don't even belong with these people," I say. "They're all useless. They're burdening the state, not me. I'm not an idiot."

"Two."

"Why are we really being moved? What are you going to do to us?"

"Three."

"Don't! Sebastian!" Emmerich says.

Frederick looks at me. His expression is expectant.

The guard steps toward me. "Four."

"No!" Emmerich says. "Come back. Tell me a story."

"What?" a woman says. "A story?"

The guard puts his gun to my chest. "Last chance."

"Wait! Can he tell a story?" a man says.

"I want to hear a story," a woman says.

I look around. Everyone stares at me. The guard's finger hugs the trigger. A nurse who's protected me from Frederick a few times walks over.

"It's not a bad idea," he says to the guard. "Let him tell a story. Just one. It'll calm everyone down."

"You can't be serious," I say.

The guard lowers his gun. "Do it," he says.

A few people shift in their seats to look at me. I glance around.

"What is wrong with you?" I say. "I'm not telling a fairy tale when there's a dead child five feet away from me."

"Please," Emmerich says. Many people assent. Some of them plead.

I feel sick. I put my hands on the seats to hold myself up. I hang my head and then groan and look at the ceiling, away from the blood.

"This is ridiculous," I say.

"What is this?" Frederick says, smacking his seat. "Just shoot him!"

"No!" Emmerich says.

"Let him tell the story!" people say. They stand and holler. The nurses approach. I pull my hair and stomp on the floor.

"Goddamn it! Once upon a time! Once upon a time, the village of Hamelin was overrun by rats!"

The bus quiets. The nurses stay where they are. The guard leans on a seat. People watch me. My voice cracks.

"Jesus," I say. "There were rats everywhere you looked in Hamelin: in the cupboards, in the beds, even in the governor's wash basin." I clear my throat. "Nobody knew what to do. The people set traps. They bought dozens of cats. They chased the rats and slashed at them with knives and shot at them with guns. Nothing worked. The rats wouldn't go away."

"Oh, I love this story," a woman says.

"Shush!" another woman says.

I take a long breath. The nurses wait.

"So the people gathered at a town meeting. They cried out, 'O what will we do about these horrible rats? What will we do? What will we do?' They couldn't come up with an answer. And then the next day, a strange man came to the village. He wore a green hat and he played a pipe."

A few people titter. Frederick mumbles to himself and turns away from me. I speak louder.

"The governor watched the strange man. As he walked throughout the town playing his pipe, the rats followed him. The governor then approached the piper and said, 'I will give you the village's treasury if you can get rid of all the rats.'"

"God, I hate rats," someone says.

"Shush!"

"Without a word, the piper began playing a whimsical tune, and immediately the rats began following him. The piper walked through every street and every alley playing his tune, and the crowd of rats grew and grew into several thousand, and once the piper had rounded up all the rats, he walked to the village gate and led them out. The gate closed behind him, and shortly he returned, and the rats were gone."

One of the nurses says something in his colleague's ear. His colleague puts his finger to his lips.

"What about the rest of it?" someone says.

My throat is dry. The disgusting smell rises. I cough. I feel weak.

"The people of Hamelin rejoiced. The piper went to the governor and said, 'I've done what you've asked of me. I'll collect my payment now.' But the governor said no. 'You agreed to give me the treasury,' the piper said. But the governor was never willing to bankrupt the village. He turned the piper away and shut himself in his office. Dejected, the piper wandered around the village, and soon came across a large group of children."

A sob catches in my throat. I swallow it down and chuckle in spite.

"The children saw the piper and said, 'Hello. Could you play a song for us?' Despite his mood, the piper could not resist an opportunity to play. He began piping a merry tune."

"Which tune?" someone says.

"Shut up!"

"The children gathered around him, and as he kept playing, more and more children joined."

"That's your fucking fantasy, isn't it?" Frederick says.

"Shush!"

"Jesus. Nobody cares even when he confesses out loud. What the fuck?"

I put my stomach into my voice. "The piper then got an idea. He began walking around the village, the same route he'd taken for the rats: every street, every alley, every walkway. Soon every child in Hamelin was following him. And the piper, sneering at the governor's office, led the children away to the gate, and one by one they left, and the gate closed, and they all disappeared behind it."

People nod. A few of them mumble questions. The nurses seem relieved.

"Can you tell another one?" a woman says.

I sag. "What about the boy?" I say.

"He'll be taken care of when we arrive," a nurse says.

"What does that mean? What will happen to the man who shot him?"

"He's being punished as we speak," the guard says.

"Punished how?"

"Appropriately."

"What? A mark on his record?"

"Go sit down," the guard says.

"Wait!" a woman says. "Can't he tell another story?"

NADJA

"It's not done. What about the parents?" Judith says.

I slide a little. My legs sink further beneath the seat. My shirt is sweaty. I feel like liquid. My hands curl over the edge. I'm bored. I want to be lifted and dangled like a puppet. I want someone to move my mouth and speak for me.

I swing my eyes over to Judith. The light falls flatly on her face. The bus hits a bump; she grabs my hand.

"The parents just let their kids be taken away?" she says.

"It's a story," I say.

Judith frowns and shakes her head. The bus' air has changed. "Nadja? Can you hear me?" She lifts my bandaged hand and squeezes it. It hurts. I pull it away.

"Stop," I say.

She takes my other hand and bows her head. Her hair is soft and brown.

"I'll watch over you," she says. "I'll watch for the both of us."

She prays again. She lifts her head for a moment and glances toward the front of the bus. She bows and speaks in a lowered voice.

"Deliver me not unto the will of my enemies. The Lord gives strength unto his people, and the Lord will bless his people with peace."

She crosses herself, as she always does. To watch her pray is heartbreaking. The sedative's making me think generously: at this moment her piousness is singular and beautiful.

EWALD

They're all suspicious of me. They think I'm a drunk and that I don't do a proper job. Perhaps they think I scrape the ashes from the bottom of the oven and put them in the urns, forsaking the right of the dead to be returned to their families. Well, let them think that, as long as they don't bring harm to Beate and Helena.

I often watch the other staff members, the young doctor in particular. He's afraid. The colour's drained from his face. One day in January, about a week after he arrived, the two of us sat in the cafeteria drinking coffee, and we asked each other what we missed about home. He told me he missed his mother's baking. I told him that I missed my family: walking down the street, playing games, going to church.

I asked him why he became a psychiatrist. He said, "I've been told I have a gift for putting myself into the minds of other people."

He sipped his coffee.

"I've always been interested in different sorts of people," he said. "When I was eight, I had a schoolmate with many behavioural problems. Everyone kept saying he hated school and was being deliberately disruptive, but I could tell he wasn't. There was something in him that drove him to shout, or smack his palm on the desk, or throw his pencil against the wall. So psychiatry seemed the best choice for me."

"What happened to that boy?" I said.

"He was taken out of school," he said. "I never saw him again."

He got up, refilled both of our coffee cups, and sat back down and told me about his education, and how the Party steered him away from conventional psychiatry into what he called a more streamlined approach.

"There's no psychiatry at all, really," he said. "The patients are all diagnosed before they come here. All we have to do is look at the file." He chuckled. "It's a bit ironic," he said, "because the people who come here have all been deemed useless, and I often wonder if I'm even needed here."

"Why do they need you here?" I said.

"Only doctors are permitted to run the shower room," he said.

"Why psychiatrists?"

"To legitimize the endeavour."

My coffee was bitter. I finished it.

"Do you regret coming here?" I said.

He looked out the window.

"How did you end up here?" he said.

"I was looking for a job," I said. "They didn't tell me my duties until I arrived."

He nodded. I peered out the window. It was a relief to see a plain grey sky.

The hospital stands on a hill, and down the hill and across the medieval bridge into town there's a church. A few days before,

I'd asked Doctor Berner if I could attend mass. He said no. I asked the young doctor if he could attend; he said no. He rocked his coffee cup from side to side. "I wonder," I said, "do we work in a hospital or a prison?" He smiled. We stared out the window. I asked him about his relationship with God. He frowned and said that although he comes from a Catholic family, he hasn't prayed or been to church in years. The last time he attended church, he went with his mother. "It was comforting," he said. "Things seemed simpler."

I stand at the bottom of the stairs, watching for shadows at the top. I quickly open my flask and drink. Like the doctor, most of the staff members have abandoned God's grace. An unofficial clause of the Party's oath is to renounce the teachings of Christ and replace them with the new German logic. The *Hitlerjugend* are especially devout in this regard; they openly chastise and harass people attending church. Anna once wrote that a good friend of hers had gone home with a broken nose.

I take a long drink, holding the liquor at the back of my throat. I tip my head back and swallow.

The fool hath said in his heart, There is no God. They are corrupt, they have done abominable works, there is none that doeth good. The Lord looked down from heaven upon the children of men to see if there were any that did understand and seek God. They are all gone aside, they are all together become filthy; there is none that doeth good. No, not one. Have all the workers of iniquity no knowledge? Who eat up my people as they eat bread, and call not upon the Lord? They were in great fear, for God is in the generation of the righteous.

They embrace the murder of so-called idiots. Yet they are all idiots in their own ways. If God is gone, not only is there no hope, no empathy, and no mercy, but there is no longer a mechanism for proper judgement. We are left alone with our pettiness. We drift apart.

The liquor nestles into my stomach. I stand up straight and wet my fingers and pull my hair into place. The hot, filthy odour from the oven swells through my nostrils.

SEBASTIAN

Robert's eyes were wide and dark. His hair was neat except in the front; he'd play with it while I told stories. He always sat at the back of the group, as though he believed that if he got too close to me, he'd be absorbed into the story.

One day, when story time had ended and the other kids scattered throughout the library, Robert waited until I sat up from the chair and walked up to me and said, "I'm a child, right?"

"Well, Robert," I said, "how old are you?"

"I'm seven."

"Then yes, you're a child."

His face turned grave. "There were children in that story," he said.

I'd just read them *The Wolf and the Seven Little Children.*

"Yes," I said, "there were children. Just young goats, though."

Robert looked at the floor and touched his hair. "Would I be the one in the clock?"

I still don't know if it was the way he said it, or if I'd been drawn to him all along, but at that moment storytelling became inadequate. It was no longer a viable way of providing the intimacy I needed; my old urgency roared back. I took him into the storeroom and made him sit on my naked lap. The smell of the books and inventory lists melded with Robert's scent. I hugged him close. I kissed the back of his head. I cupped his knees, his elbows, his buttocks. When the orgasm came, I gripped his shoulders and pulled him down toward me. It was glorious, revelatory. The storeroom brightened. The air had been blasted clean.

After that, stories were simply a way of passing the time. I no longer told them with the same vigour.

Poor, poor Thomas. He never lashed out like he did with the others on the ward. He wasn't afraid of me. He cried, but quietly, like he didn't want to be discovered. He might've been grateful for me. As I touched him, he looked like he was settling into it. I might've reminded him of a previous experience. Amidst his constant raging distress, maybe all he wanted was familiarity.

FREDERICK

I adjust the coat. Strings of the boy's blood thick as glue. Someone I think Leopold grunts vomits. His neck shaking. Another seizure. The guard's black boots. The slick tubular end of his gun. *Frederick walked out the door and down* Brienner *Straße away from the three-storey* Braunes Haus. *A short ways down the block, he stopped to examine himself in a window. He straightened his collar and brushed a hair off the skeleton key of the* Leibstandarte. *He adjusted his hat and straightened his posture.* Meine Ehre heißt Treue, *he said. A woman walked past and smiled at him. He watched her continue down the street.* The low ceiling. Everyone's sickness browns the air. Full of their shit piss vomit blood weakness. I'm breathing in their diseases. They cry for another story. An orderly looks through the curtain and says "We're almost there." "Another! Another story!" They clap. They shout. They love Sebastian. I say "Shut up!" Gruppenführer Hesse! *A* Schutzstaffel *officer ran up to him and saluted him. He held a copy of* Der Stürmer. *Take a look at this, the officer said. He opened the newspaper to a cartoon that took up half the page: a caricature of the* Führer *and Himmler grinning and standing like children on Frederick's broad shoulders as he stomped all over a map of the world with his gigantic black boots. The caption read* THE GREAT CONQUERORS. Scuffling in the back. A woman seizes Sebastian pleading for a story. Puts her hands around his neck. Sebastian pushes her away. The guard walks past me and hauls the woman back by her hair. A man stands and starts punching the guard. Two orderlies run back. The guard elbows the man in the face. *Frederick laughed. It's a very good drawing, he said. The artist really captured the sharpness of Himmler's features. Yes,* Gruppenführer. *It's refreshing to see a picture of myself in which I'm smiling rather than frowning. The officer laughed. Indeed,* Gruppenführer. *There's a rumour around headquarters you will soon reach the rank of* Reichsführer. *Wouldn't that be the day? Frederick said. It's a persistent rumour, the officer said, especially since you'd be skipping two ranks. I'd be honoured if that happened, Frederick said, but it's only a rumour, and I don't listen to rumours. Do you? No,* Gruppenführer. *In any case, there's much more work to be done. More battles to win, more ground to gain. Yes,* Gruppenführer. *You can leave this with me, Frederick said, holding up the newspaper. I have more copies upstairs, the officer said. I'll distribute them soon. I just thought you'd want to be the first one to see it. Thank you. You're dismissed. As the officer walked away, Frederick took another look at the cartoon and smiled.* A third orderly approaches. He passes me. At the front there's only one orderly left. I step into the aisle and run to the front. Tackle the last orderly shove him back. Swipe away the curtain. Bright bright light. Kick at the door. The driver yells. "Open it!" Kick the orderly in the face. Punch the driver. He brakes I lurch forward hit the window the orderly grabs my leg kick him again the other orderlies see. "Give me! Open the fucking door!" I pull the door handle jump out the bus still moving concrete grass green cool fresh breathe cool heady free run run run down the bank a river a small church trees kids down the road stop I stumble turn to the river shouting behind me no run run into the water someone behind me no I breathe wade into someone falls on top of me no pulls me hits me in the head no hits me pushes me into the water the bright rocks I kick someone slams my head into the rocks no hits me my teeth clack no chance to breathe no

EMMERICH

blood the man's nose twists, the woman cries, the man lies in the aisle knocked out, the bus has stopped, Sebastian I say Frederick's gone, the guard and the nurses at the front say everyone stay where you are sit down, where'd Frederick go why'd he get to leave, at the front two nurses bring Frederick back on the bus throw him into the aisle Frederick's wet his forehead bleeds, people chatter yell, the nurses are wet too they pull the curtain across yell at us can't you all stay quiet and stay still for ten goddamn minutes bunch of worthless vermin, Frederick's shiny wet hair makes me thirsty the bus starts again Frederick lies in the aisle, his eyes blink hard like he wants to cry his chin moves like he's cold, Sebastian chuckles and says something I don't understand, I touch his arm and say what Sebastian, he shakes his head and says it doesn't matter, another story I say, Emmerich no get off me, he pushes me off, where does the gate go I say, what gate he says, the gate in the story where does it go, just leave it alone Emmerich, please I say, where do you think it goes, I don't know, Sebastian puts his hand over his eyes which I don't like it means he doesn't want to talk, he says the rats the children do they come back, no, so what's a place where you go that you can't come back from, I think for a minute and say war, Sebastian chuckles yes yes he says an army of children off to war absolutely right Emmerich

when Klaus left he and Papa fought Papa and Mama found out about my surgery Papa told Klaus to leave, Klaus was ready though with his uniform and his papers saying he was off to save Germany not that it's worth saving he said with you two keeping Emmerich here look at him he eats so much, he's a good worker Papa said much better worker than you you'll probably get chewed up your first day of training, Klaus laughed,

Papa stood from the kitchen table, don't laugh at me he said Emmerich may be simple but he's a good man he'd make a far better soldier than you, Klaus laughed again through his teeth Emmerich would shoot himself trying to put a gun together he's a burden, you're jealous Papa said which gave me a weird feeling because I never thought anyone would be jealous of me especially not Klaus, I'm not jealous of an idiot Klaus said he's a fat ugly drain on you two so good luck keeping him, Papa slapped Klaus and told him to go to war and never come back while Mama watched and I sat in my chair in the corner of the kitchen with a biscuit in my hand trying to decide what to say wanting Klaus to go not wanting Klaus to go

Sebastian stands up the nurses tell him to sit, he looks at Thomas' body on the floor now I see his little fingers, when the bus stopped his blood moved forward along with everyone else but there was no seat to stop the blood it kept going people pulled their legs away from it it's touching Frederick's head now, the nurses shake their heads show their teeth, they don't want to look at us anymore, I wipe sweat off my head lick it off my finger thirsty hungry for a biscuit for a plate of Mama's pork schnitzel my stomach rumbles

JUDITH

The bus slows, but the shadows come quicker. They patter across the windows. We're in a town. I shake Nadja's arm. "I think we're almost there," I say.

"Wonderful," she says.

Her mouth is still loose. I help her sit straight. Everyone is talking. The nurses watch me. I move slowly.

"They said we're going to shower, right?"

She blinks. The shadows darken. Everyone's voices quicken like this morning at the other hospital. That feels like yesterday. The bus is full of dirt. I hold Nadja's hand. It's cool and soft.

"You tried to save me today," I say.

Her head goes back. I think she's waking up.

"It was pathetic," she says. "That fat troll."

I bite my lip. "I like the name you gave me," I say. "Who's Maria Schwartz?"

"It's a character I played."

"Oh."

"It was a terrible play, too. Everything was so obvious, and it was very dark."

"Dark?"

"The writer was a coward."

I watch her face. She's waking up. I put my hands together. Nadja doesn't believe that I remember my baptism. I remember the water on my head. I remember Mama's face with the blue and green windows behind her. I remember the priest's robe and how it moved when his arm swung over me. I tried to take his hand.

Nadja knocks on the window. Her hands have come alive. They're quick and sharp. She scratches the window with her thumb. I don't like the lines in her face. I look at my hands. They're filthy.

A nurse steps forward and says, "Everyone, quiet down. We've reached Hadamar. Quiet down. Quiet. We're getting off in a few minutes, so listen. I want everyone on the right side to get off first, and then the left. Once we get inside the hospital, I want the men and women to separate. Men, women, separate. Understand?"

I sit up straight. I need to prepare. My name is Judith Hoffmann. I am twenty-one years old. I will listen and do as I am asked. I am not useless. Like everyone else I was created in God's image. That is the justification Mama gave me. Mama's voice is quiet now. I will keep her quiet but close.

The bus tilts like it's going up a hill. Then everything is dark, like we're surrounded. The bus stops. The nurses stand. I hold Nadja's hand. She will protect me. I am not like the other dirty ones. I am clean. I will be the first in the shower.

The nurses move the curtain. I see a wooden wall like a barn. The driver opens the door, and a nurse picks him up and carries him out. "Now," a nurse says, "everyone on the right, stand up and follow me." We are on the right. A nurse carries the dead boy out of the bus. Two nurses take the man lying on the seat in front of us. The man with the big head turns and looks at me. There is blood on his mouth and hands and pants. He shudders. He is crying. I stand up. The other nurse and the guard pick up the loud man lying in the aisle. His eyes are small. His cheeks are red and purple. His feet drag on the floor. There is blood on the floor. We walk around it. The air is soft and cool. I want to say a prayer like when Mama and I moved into a new house. Nadja's eyes flit around. I squeeze her hand.

"I will bless the Lord at all times," I say, "and his praise shall continually be in my mouth."

The man with the big head coughs and spits blood into the dirt. There are many footprints in the dirt. Behind the bus is a wide door that has been closed. A wooden pathway leads into a brick building. Inside the brick building is a white room.

I lift Nadja's hand. "O magnify the Lord with me," I say, "and let us exalt his name together."

Nadja snaps her head back and takes a loud breath through her nose. "Christ the Lord is nothing more than a two-bit magician," she says.

MICHAEL

"Doctor Würfel."

"I know."

I stand up straight, wipe the sweat off my head, and walk with Isabella to the lobby. As I walk I hardly feel my feet on the floor. I stumble when I turn a corner. Isabella holds me by the arm; I nod and continue.

In the lobby, Benedikt stands against the wall beside Ernst. Irmgard and Pauline wait by the desk. As I've instructed them, they've moved the syringes out of sight.

"Isabella. Irmgard."

"Yes, Doctor."

"I'd like the two of you to keep the women calm. Pauline, you have the neatest writing, so I'd like you to help me with the files."

Isabella pouts. "My writing is very neat," she says as Pauline smiles and sits behind the desk.

"Benedikt. If you could keep a close eye on the men, make sure they don't become too obstreperous."

"I know my role, Doctor. Thank you."

I hear voices and footsteps coming from the garage. I take another long breath. A male nurse comes in carrying what looks like the body of a child. The head and torso are covered by a coat. Both the coat and the child's clothes are rank with blood.

"What the hell?" Isabella says.

The nurse approaches me. "Where's the crematorium?" he says quietly. I stare at him. He tightens his face and shakes the body. "Oven. Where is it? Before the others come in."

"Come with me," Irmgard says. She touches the nurse on the shoulder and both of them walk out of the lobby.

Isabella and I look at each other. A trail of blood leads toward the basement stairs.

"Jesus," I say.

"They're coming," Benedikt says.

"Should we clean this?"

"It's too late."

"Yes," I say, "clean it. Hurry."

Isabella runs to get a mop. The oven clanks beneath us.

"Doctor."

Another nurse and a *Schutzstaffel* guard carry a man into the lobby. He is wet. His cheeks are bruised. His eyes are open but inert.

"For Christ's sake," I say. "What happened? Was there a riot?"

"He almost got away. He was in the river. We caught him and brought him back."

"You couldn't have sedated him?"

"We ran out of sedative. We didn't think we'd need so much. They've always gone along with it."

"Who are you?" I say to the guard.

"He got on at the checkpoint," the nurse says. "We thought we needed him after the boy was shot."

"Shot?"

"We'll just take him downstairs."

"No! Wait. We have an intake to do. And he's still conscious. And we didn't even get the child's name."

"His name's Thomas Möller. You can check the file when they bring it in."

"Why was he shot?"

"It was an accident. It doesn't really matter though, does it?"

I stammer. "There's a procedure…"

"Maybe it's better he was shot."

"Well, you're not taking him downstairs. Just sit him against the wall. Benedikt."

Benedikt helps them with the man. The nurse and the guard leave the room. Isabella comes back in with a mop, followed by Irmgard and the other nurse. Isabella looks at the wet man and then at me.

"What is wrong with these people?" she says. "Don't they know how to do their jobs properly?" She begins mopping the blood off the floor.

"Doctor?"

I turn to Ernst.

"Should I take his picture?"

He points at the wet man.

"No," I say.

I rub my eyes. My hands tremble. More voices arise from the corridor. Someone says, "Women on that side, men on this side. Switch now. Go." Led by the nurse and the guard, a crowd of patients enters the lobby. As they enter, their voices quiet. The first one I see is a man with a swollen head. The skin at his temples is almost translucent. His eyes are red. His mouth and clothes are streaked with blood; his jaw shifts like he's captured something in his mouth and doesn't want to let it go. Behind him, another two nurses carry an unconscious man and put him against the wall next to the wet man. His eyes are swollen shut; his limbs are slack. The nurses drop him, and his head bumps on the wall and his neck cranes to the side and he settles into an uncomfortable position.

"For the love of God," I say.

A nurse approaches the desk and gives Pauline the files. As always, each of them has been marked on the front with a big red plus sign.

"Are they in alphabetical order?" she says.

"I think so."

Pauline separates the files into three stacks. Isabella and Irmgard have returned. Irmgard gives me a look. I hear a clank in the basement below. I clap my hands.

"Okay, everyone," I say. "My name is Doctor Michael Würfel. I am one of the resident psychiatrists here in Hadamar. If you could please separate to different sides of the room – men on this side, and women on this side. Line up to the table, step forward, thank you, and then you will have your picture taken."

A young girl with Down syndrome approaches the table. "When will we get to shower?" she says.

"What's your name?"

She straightens and smoothes her skirt. "Judith Hoffmann, sir. I'm twenty-one years old."

Pauline finds the file and gives it to me. Irmgard reaches into her pocket and gives the girl a piece of candy. I read the questionnaire, which was filled in months ago. Under "Diagnosis," someone's written "Down syndrome with schizophrenic tendencies." A number of other criteria follow: mainly bedridden – yes or no; very restless – yes or no; confined – yes or no; incurable physical illness – yes or no; schizophrenia – recent stage, final stage, or good remission; retardation – disability, imbecile, or idiot; epilepsy – average frequency of attacks; senile disorders – very confused or soils self. The file also lists date of birth, city, primary caregiver, residence, race, religion, nationality, cost-bearer, types of therapy, crimes committed, occupation, and whether release is expected soon. The girl standing before me was born on January twentieth, 1920. She is classified as a restless, incurable idiot with recent stage schizophrenia who sews quilts and mends dresses.

"Where's the shower? I'm very dirty."

I initial the bottom of the questionnaire and pass it to Ernst. "You'll get to shower soon enough. Right now, if you could please step over here so we can take your picture."

Isabella starts to lead the girl in front of the camera. The girl fiddles with her candy. "I've never had my picture taken before," she says. "Do I look clean enough?"

The wet man starts to get up. The guard steps on his leg and holds his gun above his head. He calls Benedikt over; they exchange a few words, and Benedikt takes a syringe and sedates the man.

Another woman approaches the desk. She stumbles a little. Her eyes are dense.

"Nadja Pabst."

Pauline gives me the file. The diagnosis reads "Delusional." Under "Primary symptoms," it says "Little or no concept of reality. Patient finds everything comedic, no matter how serious or ridiculous."

I study her for a moment. "Do you know where you are right now?" I say.

"I'm not an idiot."

"Were you sedated?"

She scoffs.

"I see you're an actor."

"I was. But the *Schweinstaffel* didn't like that. So they picked me up."

"You were born in Limburg. That's where I'm from."

"I don't belong here."

"Okay."

"When will I be released?"

"Hopefully soon. You can move along now."

"How soon is soon?"

"Soon enough."

She holds up her hand. "Can I have my bandage changed? And a tetanus shot? It's been three fucking days."

"In a while."

"Why not now?"

"We're busy right now."

"Fucking Nazis."

She moves out of the line toward the camera. I initial the file and give it to Pauline. The man with the swollen head comes forward.

"What's your name?"

"Hlee-pode."

He speaks from the corner of his mouth.

"Can you repeat that, please?"

He grimaces and lowers his head. "Hlee-pode."

"Lee-hode? I'm sorry, I can't understand you. You have something in your –"

The man opens his mouth. A ragged cache of blood falls onto the floor. Pauline slides back into me. He's nearly bitten off the end of his tongue. A rough piece of pink flesh wags over his teeth. He leans forward and says, "Leopold."

Pauline lowers her eyes. "Leopold. And your last name?"

He blinks. The skin under his eyes has been rubbed raw. He draws a "w" in the air.

Pauline gives me the file. He is an unemployed twenty-four-year-old with hydrocephaly, which has given him daily epileptic seizures – the cause, no doubt, of his severed tongue. I initial the file and think that, when I am filling out death certificates later on, it would be believable if he died of natural causes.

The line continues. As always, their ailments surprise me, because many of them appear normal. Also, the sheer diversity of afflictions makes me mourn the potential research opportunities. So much knowledge could be gleaned from these people.

Ernst takes their pictures efficiently, changing the film and adjusting the tripod when necessary. The camera's loud click and flash give the intake a particular rhythm, into which the staff and I, and, following us, the patients, settle. Many of them ask for water; Isabella brings them small cups. Irmgard continues giving the young ones candy. Some of the adults ask for candy; she obliges.

Once their pictures have been taken, the patients retreat to different sides of the room: the men stand by the windows, the women by the plain white wall. Eventually, the Scheuern nurses lift up the two beaten men and bring them to Pauline and I. I nod at the wet man.

"Frederick Hesse," a nurse says.

I read his file. No work skills and no occupation to speak of; diagnosed as sociopathic with frequent episodes of megalomania; symptoms include laziness, lack of empathy, flagrant lying, and violent fits. Under "Crimes committed," someone has written "Theft, loitering, lying to officers of the law, disturbing the peace, fighting, stalking and lewd behaviour, destruction of public property, and unusual cruelty to animals." I study the man. He hasn't shaved in days. His black hair is dense and shiny. He has difficulty keeping his eyes open. The nurses take him to the other side of the room; the guard follows. I initial the file, and the next man's brought forward.

"Peter Duerden."

A former lawyer, he is listed as a depressed psychotic. Symptoms include sexual deviancy and complete ignorance of reality. His eyes have been beaten shut. A note reads, "Patient was originally committed after walking into a market naked and wiping his rear end with a potato." He was sterilized last year. The nurses take him away. A tall young man approaches the table. Every few seconds, he glances back at the older man standing behind him.

"What's your name?"

"Emmerich."

"Last name?"

He looks back at the older man, who looks away. The young man pouts.

"Van Mandelhoven," he says.

He has been diagnosed as an idiot. He's worked on a farm training horses, carrying grain, milking cows, and making deliveries. A note at the bottom reads that, like Mr. Duerden, he's been sterilized.

"Move over there, please," I say.

The man looks back at his companion. "Go on, Emmerich," says the older man. He looks fatigued, as though he's taken care of the young man for a long time.
"Your name, please."

"Sebastian Brendelbeck."

I open the file. Pedophilia, indecent exposure. He's a librarian. Under "Remarks," someone's written, "People like this are an embarrassment and a burden to the German people."

"Why have we been moved here?" he says.

"For administrative reasons," I say.

"What sort of reasons?"

"They needed the room at Scheuern."

"How many beds do you have here?"

"Enough. Over a hundred."

"Where are all the other patients?"

"They're in the next wing."

"Where was the boy taken? The one who was shot?"

"Move along, please," Benedikt says, touching Mr. Brendelbeck on the shoulder.

Mr. Brendelbeck studies me.

"Please, Mr. Brendelbeck," I say.

"Why are we here?" he says.

"He just explained," Benedikt says. "Now move on."

Mr. Brendelbeck sighs and joins the others in line by the camera, where Ernst is adjusting the height for the tall man, Emmerich.

Once everyone has been photographed, Pauline collects the files and takes them out of the lobby. Ernst breaks down the camera and puts it in its box. Benedikt, Isabella, Irmgard, and the other nurses manage the patients. A nurse from Scheuern approaches me. "Do we still need the guard?"

"No. Leave him there. Actually, tell him to go outside."

"Are you sure?" he whispers. "He has a gun."

"He's frightening the patients. I don't want him in here." I back out of the lobby and glance down the hall. There's no more blood on the floor. I step back in and say, "Everyone, may I have your attention please? Everyone? Please, be quiet. Quiet down. Now that we've gone through the paperwork, it's time for you to shower." Judith, the girl with Down syndrome, exclaims. "Now, this may seem a bit unorthodox, but we're going to ask you all to shower together, both men and women. So you'll need to remove your clothing, please, and put it in a pile in the middle of the room. We'll then give each of you a coat to put on that you can wear downstairs."

EWALD

They drop the body on the floor and go back upstairs. I don't give myself a chance to stare. I open the oven door and lift the boy onto the rails. His body is too thin; the rails are too wide. I prop his neck on the left rail and his legs on the right and push him inside with the poker and close the door and step away. I walk to the end of the hall, staying close to the wall, away from the blood.

Every time a bus arrives, I picture Beate among the patients. I picture her huddled in her seat, her hands over her eyes, crying and making little hiccupping noises. She's frightened. The people around her scare her. She wants nothing more than to be with her mother and father. Because she can't properly articulate herself, everyone on the bus either humours her or ignores her. They hustle her into the hospital and rush her through the intake. She fights to keep her clothes on; she's offended when a nurse tries to undress her. She fights to stay in the lobby. She fights all the way down to the shower room, elbowing and punching and scratching at anyone who approaches her. She cowers on the checked shower room floor; she clings to someone's leg. She cries, and as the gas builds in the room, her sobs become more pronounced and irregular. She dies crying, afraid and alone.

They've all gathered upstairs. I take a long drink from my flask and resume what the nurses interrupted. I put my hands together and bow my head and pray that God extends His mercy to all those who go into the shower room today so that they are not afraid and so that they die without much pain. I pray that my wife remains strong and that my daughter is not found and that she is not killed by the Nazis. I pray that the doctor and the rest of the staff will one day see the cruel and heinous nature of their actions. I pray that God forgives my many weaknesses.

I stand up straight and take another sip from my flask. My hands shake. They'll be coming down any minute now. I move closer to the oven, out of sight from the hallway. I try to keep Beate out of my mind.

LEOPOLD

I want to ask why we need to have a shower right this minute when all I want to do is for my pain to stop. I try to get the doctor's attention, but he's busy directing everyone. My mouth is full. I let more blood fall on the floor. People move away from me. I cry. I can't stand their voices.

The women turn the other way and jostle, trying to hide behind each other. The nurses keep the men and women separate. One of the men seizes a woman from behind and tries to shove his penis into her, saying "Let me fuck you, just for a minute." He thrusts his hips toward her. The woman whimpers and slaps him. One of the male Hadamar nurses hauls him back to this side of the room. The man persists; the nurse shoves him against the wall and kicks him in the groin. The man cries out and doubles over. I wince. Another Hadamar nurse tries to help me undress. I'm exhausted. I neither cooperate nor resist. He unbuttons my shirt and my trousers. I let him undress me. He puts a heavy military coat on my shoulders. I sag and lean against the wall. I leave my mouth open and let the blood fall out. Neither the nurse nor the doctor seems to care.

If I say something, everyone will panic, and things will slow down even more.

Everyone's voices fill my head. I sway on my feet.

Is this what Aunt Minna wanted for me when she gave me up? Did she see me being put through all this? I never knew how she and Uncle Helmut decided. I imagine Aunt Minna thought that I put her in danger because of my condition. In her mind, we were equally vulnerable, so giving me up to the *Schutzstaffel* was the most reassuring thing she and Uncle

Helmut could do. It'd show their willingness to cooperate and would divert attention from her. I imagine that Uncle Helmut didn't agree, that Aunt Minna had to act on her own, which would've been risky due to her deafness. Uncle Helmut couldn't choose between his wife and his nephew, nor could he endanger us both. He probably hoped he could hide me for as long as he needed, but Aunt Minna didn't want to wait any longer. Her anxiety exhausted her.

The doctor checks the files and continues giving instructions. The nurses keep telling everyone to take off their clothes and put on their coats. They don't let anyone lag behind. Despite my headache, I feel comforted for the moment. The doctor's thoroughness and the nurses' efficiency make me think that Aunt Minna will be picked up too. I pull my coat tighter around myself. I feel sad for Uncle Helmut, who'll end up alone.

I close my eyes and try humming again. I cry a little. I don't want to move. They can kill me where I stand. A few people yell. Someone takes me by the hand and starts leading me forward. I let the front of my coat fall open.

JUDITH

I put on my coat and step out from behind Nadja. We're going to shower soon. I'll be clean soon. I walk to the front so I can be the first in the shower.

The others are much slower. They talk. A few of them hum. I flap the long arms of my coat.

"When can we go in?" I say.

"Just a minute," says the nurse who gave me candy.

I hold out my hand. "Can I have another?"

"I'm sorry. I'm all out," she says.

"Can I go then? I'm ready."

"Just wait a minute," the nurse says.

I look back. "Come on, Nadja."

She puts her arms in the air. Her sleeves are long too. "I feel ridiculous," she says.

A man with his pants around his ankles says something to the doctor. I flap my arms. The doctor steps forward.
"Everyone please follow me," he says.

I stand right behind him and start to walk.

"We didn't have to take off our clothes back in Scheuern," says the man with his pants around his ankles.

The doctor looks back. I look back. The man doesn't move. It's the same man who told the story. His pants are still around his ankles. He's still wearing his shirt. My arms and legs are itchy and dirty. I flap my arms harder.

"Be quiet," I say. "Let's go."

"Are the wards co-ed too?" the storyteller says.

The doctor shakes his head. "This is purely for the sake of expedition," he says. "All new patients have to go through this. It's standard procedure."

"It wasn't like that in Scheuern."

"It's easier to clean you all as a group than to have you clean yourselves individually."

The storyteller puts his hands on his hips. One of the nurses stands beside him and tells him to hurry. I nod. Nadja looks around.

"Hurry up," the nurse says.

"No," the storyteller says. "I won't do this."

"Come on!" I say. I flap my arms harder.

Another man tries to grab a woman. I think it's Anna. Anna screams. The man shakes her breasts up and down. A nurse punches the man. I look at the doctor. He stands there and watches.

"Can I please go?" I say.

Another nurse tries to take the storyteller's shirt off. "Step out of your pants," he says.

"No," the storyteller says. "I won't be humiliated any longer. What happened on that bus was an atrocity."

The man tries to pull his pants back up. The nurse slaps his hands away.

"This is a gross violation of our privacy," the man says.

He tries to pull up his pants again. The nurse kicks him. The tall man steps forward. He starts choking the nurse. I see the tall man's penis through the opening in his coat. I turn away. I look at him again. I haven't seen a naked man before. His penis moves side to side. It's much bigger than the other men's. He fights the nurse. Two other nurses grab his arms. The nurse who gave me candy runs up and gives him a needle. The storyteller stumbles backward and falls. He looks around like he's scared and angry. He says something I don't hear. Everyone's talking. The nurses point toward the doctor. The doctor waves for us to follow him.

"Come on!" I say. "Come on, Nadja."

The tall man's knees shake. Two nurses take his arms and help him sit down on the floor. I can still see his penis. I turn to the doctor.

"I want to shower," I say.

"One minute," he says.

"But I'm ready. I'm ready now!"

People shout behind me. I stay where I am to show I'm ready. Nadja says something. I turn around and tell everyone to hurry.

"Fuck you, Judith."

"Shut up, Nadja. You're slowing everything down."

"Go to hell, you fucking idiot."

I start crying. A nurse puts her hand on my shoulder. I face the doctor again.

"Please don't inject me," I say. "I just want to get clean. I'm sorry."

"Don't cry, Judith."

"I'm sorry, Mama."

"I'll take her down," says a nurse. "Come with me."

She puts her arm around me. She takes me past the doctor down the hallway. We turn and there's a door. There are stairs going down.

"The shower's down there?" I say.

"Yes."
The nurse takes me down. There's a bad smell. I feel heat. I pinch my nose.

"Is that all the filth?" I say. "From everyone?"

"Yes."

We get to the bottom of the stairs. There's another hallway. We walk a little ways and turn left into a little room.

"In there," the nurse says. "You can take off your coat."

I take off my coat and give it to her. She pulls open a heavy door. There's another little room with a black and white floor. I go inside. Shower pipes across the ceiling. I look around.

"Where's the soap?" I say. "Where's the handle? For the water?"

"Just wait here a moment," the nurse says.

She goes away. I hold out my hands and wait for the water.

MICHAEL

I motion to Benedikt. "Could you and a few others take those two men downstairs first? Just so they don't interrupt." Benedikt and three other nurses lift up the beaten men. Mr. Hesse slurs and drools. I look at my watch. It's nearly twelve o'clock. Some of the women's bodies are very beautiful. A few of them whistle at the tall man, Mr. Van Mandelhoven, saying, "Look at him. With all that size. My god."

A few minutes pass. Benedikt and the others return and take Mr. Van Mandelhoven's arms and legs and carry him down; when they come back up, they're all sweating heavily. Isabella, Irmgard, and I arrange the patients into a single file; then, after placing nurses at the front and back of the line, I lead everyone downstairs. I walk around the corner down the hall and around another shorter corner to the narrow concrete stairwell. The warm odour meets me before I descend. "Watch your step," I say. The patients groan at the smell. One of them resists. "I don't like basements." The nurses keep her in the line. Everyone follows me: Isabella, Pauline, and Irmgard, then the patients, then the male nurses at the rear.

At the bottom of the stairs, we face the main hallway, sparsely lit by plain bulbs fixed in the ceiling. To our right are the ovens, concealed by a wall. Benedikt stands in front of the wall, folding his arms. Up ahead and to the left is a small room. I step aside and let the nurses guide the patients into the small room and then into the shower room. I just see its heavy metal door from where I stand. Isabella and Irmgard take their posts beside it and herd the patients inside.
"What's down there?" Mr. Brendelbeck says.

He glances over Benedikt's shoulder.

"Keep going," Benedikt says.

"What is that disgusting smell?"

"Go on."

Mr. Brendelbeck's lip wavers. He glances around the corridor, keeping his hands over his penis. He stamps his bare feet on the concrete. "You can try threatening me, but I won't go in that room."

Benedikt looks at the other male nurses. Two of them seize Mr. Brendelbeck by the arms. He pushes back against them.

"No," he says. "You can't do this. Don't make me go in there."

He tries to pull his arms away. The nurses shake him loose and coerce him into the shower room. I watch the others walk inside. The threshold is so plain, so prosaic. A strange sort of gravity beckons from the room. It'd be easy to step inside with the patients.

"Doctor!" I jar. Benedikt pants. "Go!"

I go further down the hall to the room on the other side of the shower room. The metal door here is closed; I see the patients through a small, round window. Some of them stand idly while others push each other. The one with Down syndrome is crying and holding out her hands, waiting for the water to fall from the pipes above. I ensure the door is locked. A few patients see me and knock on the window. Behind them, Benedikt keeps shoving Mr. Brendelbeck into the room. Mr. Van Mandelhoven's splayed out in a corner. People stand all around him; a few prod him with their toes. Mr. Brendelbeck tries again to escape – Benedikt punches him. As Mr.

Brendelbeck lumbers back, holding his eye, the door on the other side closes.

I move away from the window and sit in the corner, out of view. The patients' voices are muffled. Out in the hall, Benedikt says, "Just do it, Doctor! What are you waiting for?" I stand up and look through the window. Mr. Brendelbeck rests on his knees; the girl with Down syndrome shakes her arms, waiting for the water; Ms. Pabst stares at the floor, her arms folded. Mr. Hesse and Mr. Duerden rest in a corner, still fully clothed. A few men grope the women, who struggle against them. Mr. Brendelbeck sees me and gets up from his knees. I step back and put my hand on the valve. Mr. Brendelbeck knocks on the door. "What are you doing?" he says. I face away from him and quickly turn the valve. "What are you doing?" I concentrate on my watch. For the first fifteen seconds, their voices are normal, and then they rise and rise into a scathing soprano. They batter the door. I look at the window for a second and see some of them sticking their tongues out. Their eyes bulge. One of them makes noises to himself, testing his voice as though the lack of air has given him a new one. Then he shrieks and jumps up and down. Some of them punch each other. I look for the two beaten men, but they're obscured; I see only their feet. The hydrocephalic man stands in a corner, a look of relief on his face; the girl with Down syndrome shakes Ms. Schnitzler by the shoulders; Mr. Brendelbeck beats on the door. He grits his teeth. His eyes strain and reach for me. I gag and step away again. I look at my watch and turn on the carbon monoxide. I keep my eyes on the wall. They continue to pound on the door. Someone screams "No! Get off!" Their voices rise again into high-pitched hisses. I keep my trembling hands together and focus on the white wall.

Their voices diminish. The pounding slows. I begin to hear soft thuds. Some of them make small taps when they fall, like the footsteps of children. A few of them yelp and wheeze. I look at the window. All I see is a churning white cloud. A shadow moves through it. I refocus on the wall. There's a heavy knock. "Open!" the girl with Down syndrome says. Her eyes are startlingly wide. She knocks again. I wince and hold my hand to my mouth. I sniffle.

I wait ten more minutes. After the last person falls, I wait another ten minutes, and then I stand up and walk stiffly up to the window. Everyone is on the floor. They lie in strange, even erotic, positions. Heads sit facedown in laps. Hands rest on breasts. Feet cradle penises. Some of them have voided their bladders or their bowels. Some of them bleed from scratches and punches. I turn off the carbon monoxide and restore the oxygen. Their eyes are wide open. Their bodies are ruddy, like they've spent a day in the sun. Some of their bellies are swollen. For a brief moment, I wonder if pushing on their bellies would yield a sound or a white cloud. I shudder and shake the thought from my mind.

"Well?"

I turn. Ewald stands at the doorway with the trolley.

"Are you finished?"

I nod.

"How was it?"

I take a long breath. "Did you dispose of that boy?"

"Yes. The poor child was shot."

My hands are still shaking. I open and close them.

Ewald brings in the trolley. One of the wheels on the trolley is loose. It makes a sharp squeaking noise. Ewald approaches the shower room door.

"Don't open it yet," I say.

"I know."

"Of course. I'm sorry."

"You can go upstairs now, if you want."

I nod. I stay where I am for a minute. I look through the window at the bodies.

"Ewald?"

"Yes, Doctor?"

My mouth is dry. I wave my hand and leave the room and walk up the narrow stairway. I seem to float up the steps.

In the lobby, the desk has been pushed against the wall and the patients' clothes have been removed. I lean on the wall and vomit. Isabella comes around the corner.

"Are you okay?"

I grunt and wipe my mouth.

"Was it so horrible?" she says.

"Are the files in the office?"

"Yes. But why don't you wait for a while? Why don't you take a walk? You look even greyer than this morning."

"I just want to finish."

"The files can wait. You should go for a walk and get some real air. Here. Come get a drink of water."

She leads me down the hall to the washroom and gives me a cup of water.

"Now go for a little walk. It's cool outside. It'll help."

I watch her walk down the hall and disappear around the corner. I go to my room and take off my white coat. I look around at my bed and my books. My room feels infected. I put on my suit jacket and hustle down the hall and out the back door. The air is cool. I breathe extravagantly. I walk down the path past the garage. A number of small, gravel-pocked piles of snow frame the road. I choose the tree-heavy path leading past the front of the hospital. Despite the remnants of snow, the trees have begun to flourish. I walk slowly under them. I feel light-headed.

A woman smiles as she walks past me. At the end of the block, a group of children runs across the street. A soft wind slides past. Someone shouts, and I turn. I see nobody behind me. On my shoulder sits a tuft of ash and four strands of singed hair. I shake them off and look up. Ashes are drifting down all around me. The black smoke forms a ragged arch in the sky. Groaning, I cover my head and run back toward the hospital.

ACKNOWLEDGEMENTS

Kimmy Beach, for her pinpoint editorial suggestions and warm companionship.

Dennis E. Bolen and Gary Barwin, for their support.

Luciano Iacobelli, Allan Briesmaster, and the staff at Quattro, for publishing this story that took me so long to share with the world.

Uta George, Patrick Weidemann, and the staff at Gedenkstätte Hadamar, for generously showing me around, giving me access to the original patient files, and answering all my questions.

Ian Kluge, for his consistent encouragement and wonderful company.

John and Toni Stepp, for supporting this book from its initial drafts onward.

Mum, Dad, and Taylor.

Debbie. Always.

Other Recent Quattro Fiction